MAVERICKS:
MESQUITE MANHUNTERS

LONGRIDERS OF THE WEST ™

MAVERICKS

LANCE CLAYTON•DOC GRIMSON•CHARLIE PARR•LOCKJAW JOHNSON•FLINT MADDOX

MESQUITE
MANHUNTERS

By Kent Thorn

POPULAR PUBLICATIONS • 2018

PUBLISHING HISTORY

"Mesquite Manhunters" originally appeared in the October 1934 issue of *Mavericks* magazine (Vol. 1, No. 2). Copyright 1934, 1961 by Popular Publications, Inc. All Rights Reserved.

CHAPTER 1
FRIENDLY JOE TARBELL

FIVE MEN lay in some low brush at the side of the stage road between Jackson Corners and Tarpaulin. Dust-covered, they resembled gray cocoons more than men. The noon sun beat down on them like the stroke of a brazen hammer. Mud streaked their faces and hands where the sweat ran in streams through the gray dust. Red ants made laborious journeys over them and on them. Except for occasional turnings of their heads, they lay motionless.

On the road in front of them was an opened saddlebag, with a torn strap hanging from it, and by its side a leather poke, with gold dust spilling out into the road. In the fierce blaze of the sun, the gold glinted like fire.

Except for these five, the valley, which stretched out level as a billiard table to the stark hills on either side, appeared deserted. The only movement was the shimmering dance of the heat haze and the stately circling of two buzzards high overhead.

One of the men, large, barrel-chested and somewhat horse-faced, shifted his position and groaned dismally. "Them fellers ain't ever comin'," he grumbled, wiping the muddy sweat from his eyebrows with a hand which was equally muddy and sweaty.

"Stay still, you dumb galoot! You're shaking all that dust off you."

The man who said that had a flowing white mustache and

1

remarkably young-looking eyes in a seamed and wrinkled countenance

"Shucks, Charlie!" the first man protested. "What do we want to be layin' here tryin' to look like mounds of dirt for? We could just crack down on one of the horses and then go up an' hold 'em up. That's easy enough."

"Doc's running this show, Lockjaw," Charlie Parr told him. "Maybe you better let him run it."

The man referred to—Doc Grimson—turned luminous gray

eyes on the first speaker. "This sheriff, Bogart, is plenty poison-ous, Lockjaw," he said. "And the two guards on that stage are both good men. They're sworn to shoot, even if somebody has the drop on 'em. So we better play it easy and careful."

Lockjaw Johnson snorted a little but was silent.

Lance Clayton, big-shouldered, young, whose face narrow-ly escaped being handsome, expressed his silent thought for him. "How come this star-toter packs such a mean rattle?" he asked skeptically. "He ain't famous in my home town."

Doc Grimson smiled grimly. "He's plenty famous here. I never did see people so buffaloed by a name as the hombres I talked to yesterday in Jackson Corners. According to them, he's chained lightning with a six-gun and don't know what it is to be scared. He's got this county where he wants it."

"Doc's right, we got to be careful. If we have to start shootin', a lot of innocent people are goin' to get hurt." It was Flint Maddox, his features a melancholy mask under the coated dirt, who said that.

Lance Clayton asked: "You sure Bogart didn't bank that ten thousand in Jackson Corners, Doc?"

"Not likely," Doc assured him. "Bogart owns the bank in Tarpaulin. He'll be bringing it back there."

Lance nodded. He had been thinking of Flint Maddox when he asked the question. He knew Flint didn't like the idea of this hold-up, and there wasn't much use in going through with it unless Bogart was really carrying the money.

Not that Flint Maddox would ever have voiced an objection to the scheme. His loyalty to Doc would prevent that. For they were staging this hold-up to get money to help the old partner of Doc's gambling days—Friendly Joe Tarbell.

THE TWO had parted years before, when Doc Grimson began to ride the Owlhoot Trail. Friendly Joe had an only daughter, whom he worshipped, and he had stuck to gambling—honest gambling—for her sake. But the two had parted friends, and once when Doc Grimson had needed help as badly as a man can, Joe Tarbell had come to his aid.

Now, it was Friendly Joe who needed help. He had settled

in Tarpaulin and set about accumulating enough money to buy a spread of his own so that when his daughter came back from school she would find her father a respectable rancher instead of a gambler. Doc could see again the worried scrawl of Friendly Joe's letter:

I've had a lot of funny hard luck lately, but I managed to get together the money for the last payment on that spread I've been buying for the little girl—$10,000. On my way to pay up, somebody bent a six-gun over my head, and that's the last I've seen of the *dinero*. If I don't find that much in a week I lose the ranch and everything I've put into it. The kid's coming home now pretty soon. Looks like she won't find much waiting for her; unless you can let me have ten thousand.

Maybe I could pay you back sooner than you think because I've got a pretty good idea of where the money went to. There's a skunk here named Bogart and he's the one who stands to benefit if I can't pay up on time. He gets the ranch just like he's already got the money unless I'm guessing wrong—and I'm not! He slipped up a little and I've got some proof on him. He's crooked as a dog's hind leg but he's the sheriff here and too strong for me to call him, unless I can get sure proof and have somebody to back my hand. I'm working on him and I'm going to have the deadwood on him soon.

Yours,

Joe.

P.S.—I don't know yet if he knows how much I know, but if anything happens to me, Doc, I'm asking you to look after my girl.

That last sentence had been eloquent. Joe Tarbell was not the man to lose his nerve over nothing. It meant that he needed another sort of help in addition to money, and needed it worse than he was willing to say.

Well, Lance thought, setting his jaw, he would get it. There wasn't one of them who wouldn't back Doc Grimson's play to the limit, and Doc could generally be counted on to accomplish what he set out to do. It had been a stroke of genius on his part to locate Sheriff Bogart in Jackson Corners, where he had just been paid in cash for a herd of cattle, and to plan to take away from him the money which Joe Tarbell needed.

"Here she comes!" said Charlie Parr, suddenly.

"Take your sombreros off, boys," said Doc Grimson quietly, "and put 'em under you, then pile dust in your hair and keep your heads down."

Lance obeyed, his heart beginning to pound a little. The cover afforded by the low, sparse brush was almost no cover at all. Their only chance was to blend with the ground and keep completely still. The flicker of an eye-lash at the wrong moment would attract attention and send the guards' lead ripping into them.

CHAPTER 2
SHERIFF BOGART SLIPS

ALMA BLAKE, in her corner of the Jackson Corners-Tarpaulin stage, watched the man opposite her covertly and felt an unaccountable nervous shiver under her breastbone. The feeling surprised her, for, while she did not like Sheriff Ben Bogart, there was no good reason why she should be afraid of him. Theoretically, she ought to feel safer with him than with anybody else. He stood for law and order as few men ever had.

If, for example, the stage in which she rode was in no danger of being held up, that was largely due to Ben Bogart. It was he who had been responsible for clearing away the few spots of cover which the level smoothness of the valley floor had once offered to hold-up men. It was he who had hired the two guards, now on the boot, who were sworn to go down shooting before they allowed the stage to be robbed. And it was he who had cleaned up Blood Mountain County so thoroughly that few outlaws were bold enough to operate there.

Wealthy cattleman, mine-owner, banker and lawman, Ben Bogart had his own methods of getting rid of undesirables. If he had evidence enough, he arrested his man; if not, he killed him or warned him to leave the country. It was said that nobody, so far, had had to be warned twice.

Looking at him now, she felt that she understood why. Hunched in his corner, staring out of the window on the vacant landscape with brooding, implacable eyes, he appeared suddenly sinister to her—not so much a man as a naked force of will, stripped of everything which might conceivably hinder its mysterious purposes. Violent, ruthless, insatiable in his lust for power.

That unpleasant impression was broken by a sudden slackening of the coach, which came, after a moment, to a halt.

Bogart put his head out of the window. "What's the matter, Jim?" he asked sharply.

"Something kind of funny in the road, Sheriff," the driver's voice came respectfully in reply. "Looks like a saddlebag an'—"

"Holy Smokes!" one of the guards broke in. "It's gold!"

Alma could hear him get down hurriedly from the boot, followed by the sound of the other guard alighting. The sheriff leaned farther out of the window in an attempt to get a sight of whatever it was. An instant later, she saw him start and then freeze. Simultaneously, a vibrant, imperative voice came to her. "Get 'em high, gents!"

A fraction of a second of stunned silence greeted the words. During that space, Alma became acutely aware of a number of things—of hands groping carefully upward, of the suddenly opened eyes of her little girl who had been asleep in her arms, of the sheriff's fist, white-knuckled on the window, and of the terror-stricken face of the fat man on the other side of the coach. It was funny to see him now, she thought abstractedly, with the color drained from his fat lips and his eyes starting out of his head. He looked quite different from the coarse, soft-looking man who had tried at first to flirt with her in a furtive sort of way.

Almost before the thought flashed through her mind, a double report from the front of the coach smashed the stillness.

Just one double report, followed by a momentary confusion of cursing that had a note of deep surprise in it, a sharp warning voice saying, "Hold 'em!" and the snorts and tattooing hoofs of scared horses.

A big-shouldered man appeared at the window, a bandanna masking his face and a pair of cocked six-guns in his hands.

"You may be a brave man, pardner," he said to the sheriff in a pleasant musical voice which somehow convinced her that he was young, "but there's no use in forcing me to cut you down. Just lean back from the window with your hands up and come out, quiet and careful, when I open the door."

THE SHERIFF hesitated before his back muscles relaxed and he leaned away from the window with his hands raised. Alma could see his eyes now, and the concentrated fury in them startled her.

There was another man on the opposite side of the coach, also with two Colts in his hands. He said nothing.

A third man appeared and opened the door. Ben Bogart stepped out. The other passengers followed him—all but Alma and the fat man in the far corner. At the sight of Alma, the robber who had opened the door made a little gesture of surprise and concern.

"Mighty sorry to trouble you, ma'am," he said apologetically.

The silent man on the other side of the coach said contemptuously to the fat man: "Go on, you—git out! We ain't gonna do nothin' but cut the heart out of you—an' there'll be enough remains for the sky-pilot to make his spiel over, so you got nothin' to worry about!"

Alma got to her feet awkwardly, because of the little girl in her arms, and started to get out. The highwayman who had opened the door holstered his guns hastily and stepped forward to help her. The pleasant-voiced young man was disarming the rest of the passengers and herding them up toward the head of the coach. The big man on the other side circled the stage to help him.

"Let me take the little lady, ma'am," the third robber said, extending his arms.

Automatically, Alma held the child out to him, without stopping to wonder why he did not arouse distrust in her. The highwayman gathered Julie in his hard-muscled embrace with extraordinary gentleness. His eyes, Alma saw, were brown and filled with something very like wistfulness. Perhaps because she was watching them, and wondering, Alma set her foot in a rut as she stepped down, and fell, twisting her ankle. The robber set Julie down hurriedly, and went to help her up.

"Did you hurt yourself?" His tone was concerned, and remorseful—as though he were somehow to blame.

"It's nothing," Alma told him, forcing a smile. "I'm all right."

The robber bent down and began to comfort Julie, who, seeing her mother fall, had begun to cry.

Out the corner of her eye Alma saw the fat man thrust his hand under his coat. It came out, fumblingly, holding a short-barrelled, ugly-looking gun. His eyes were glazed.

For an instant, astonishment held her paralyzed. The fat man trained the gun on the stooping highwayman. His hand shook, then steadied. Alma cried out then.

She did not stop to think that she was aiding a bandit against the law. The cry was torn from her throat instinctively. "Look out! He's going to—"

The robber whirled, hand streaking for a holstered Colt, just as the fat man squeezed the trigger. The outlaw's gun leapt from the holster, belching sudden thunder. The fat man's smoking, short-barrelled gun fell from his right hand, while his left clutched at a shattered shoulder. He began to scream in a frightened, high-pitched voice, like that of a woman.

Alma realized that he had been beside himself with fear, otherwise he would never have found the courage to go for his gun. Now his nerve had broken entirely. His screams had a horrifying, animal-like quality. Julie began to cry. It was pandemonium.

The big, silent man had come leaping at the first shot. Now he reached into the coach and yanked the fat man out. "You snake!" he snarled. "I ought to wring your neck!"

"Easy! Easy!" the man who had fired the shot cautioned. "He's hurt."

"Not as bad as he's going to be if he tries anything more! Shut up that noise, you!"

The fat man subsided and began to whimper. The big man marched him off to join the others. The other stooped and picked Julie up in his arms. "Don't you be scared, honey," he said remorsefully. "Don't you be scared."

But the child was scared. Frantically, she beat at the outlaw's face, wanting to be put down. One of her hands caught in his bandanna, pulled it down.

Alma gasped. Unmasking robbers, even friendly ones with kind voices, was not, she supposed, an exactly safe thing to do. But the man, though he looked momentarily startled, did not appear vexed. He was standing with his back to the others and made no immediate attempt to replace the mask.

She saw that he was a homely man, with big features that had an indefinable air of sadness about them, even when they were lighted by tenderness, as they were now when he looked at Julie. And oddly, now that his face was uncovered, Julie stopped crying.

THE ROBBERY of the other passengers, meanwhile, was going forward with dispatch and according to somewhat curious rules. The slender, quiet-voiced man who conducted it seemed to be able to find nothing that he wanted. He examined the wallets and watches the passengers produced for him in a cursory way and then returned them indifferently to their owners.

Alma saw with surprise that the two guards appeared uninjured. She had expected to find them dead, for her range-bred ears had told her that those first two shots had not been fired by rifles but by revolvers. Now she saw the two Winchesters lying in the road, the walnut stock of one of them smashed by a bullet. They must have been shot from the hands of the guards.

For a moment the significance of that did not reach her, then she stared at the slender man and at a fifth robber in astonishment. They must have been the two who had done that. What kind of highwaymen were these who would take a chance on shooting the weapons out of men's hands instead of shooting the men themselves?

The slender man came to Bogart at that moment. "Will you produce it all for us?" he asked quietly, "or shall I go over you for it?"

She could see that Bogart's anger burned white-hot in him, but he said nothing. He reached in the inner pocket of his coat and drew out a bulging wallet. The slender man opened it, extracted a thick sheaf of banknotes which he ran through with expert fingers as though estimating their value, and then returned the wallet itself to Bogart.

"About $10,000?" he remarked inquiringly.

The sheriff made no answer. He was white to the lips.

The slender man shrugged and stowed the bills away in his pocket. One of the robbers had gone off toward a thicket and he returned now, mounted and leading four horses.

The fifth man, whose dust-covered hair under his sombrero looked as though it might be white, gathered up the guns belonging to the passengers and the guards and tossed them into the brush.

The man who had held Julie came up and stuck a hard, rough finger out to her. "So-long, Missy," he said, his eyes smiling. "Don't you be scared of anything." And then he turned to Alma, somewhat shyly. "Good-bye an' good luck, ma'am."

"Mighty sorry to have bothered you, ma'am." It was the big-shouldered young man with the musical voice who said that to her as he strode toward his horse.

Bogart heard him and said grimly: "You'll have plenty of other regrets before I'm through with you!"

The highwayman laughed.

"Don't get too anxious to jump for those guns," he advised.

A moment later they were in the saddle, riding at an easy lope toward the great, bare, red and orange bulk of Blood

Mountain, stark against the metallic blue of the noon-day sky. None of them, Alma observed, looked back, except the man with the sad-looking brown eyes. He turned once and waved— to Julie, no doubt.

BEN BOGART stood rooted, until the group of riders had traversed perhaps a hundred yards, then he came violently to life.

"Get your guns and get in to your places," he yelled, his face contorted. He jumped into the brush and began tossing their weapons back to the passengers and guards. Then he rushed at the driver and the guards, yammering at them to get started. He turned and charged back toward the passengers, shooing them into the coach as though they were chickens.

Alma saw that the man was really beside himself, temporarily a madman. The blaze in his eyes had an almost physical power of compulsion. The others gave back before it, bewildered. Confused, dominated, they piled into the coach before her, forgetting their ordinary rough but unfailing courtesy.

Alma herself was so occupied by the spectacle that she forgot to move. It came to her in a flash that she was witness to an unveiling of the man's true character. The thing before her was an ego, dangerously swollen, flicked to the raw by an incident which would have left a normally modest man untouched.

Alma thought: he's making himself ridiculous, but God help those men if he ever strikes their trail!

She saw that the driver was in his place and that she was the only one holding things up. Bogart rushed at her with his head down, bellowing like a bull. "Get in—get in," he roared, plucking her by the elbow and giving her a shove toward the door.

Half-angry, half-tempted to laugh, she moved toward the door, put her foot on the step and started to mount. It would be hours before Bogart would take the trail with a posse; what did a few seconds now matter?

"Let 'em go!" Bogart yelled. The driver waited, looking back to see that Alma and the child in her arms were safely in. Bogart, evidently supposing that she had gotten aboard, cursed and yelled and ran toward the horses. He brought his palm down resoundingly on the hind-quarters of the near-wheeler and leapt forward like a maniac, fanning the leaders with his sombrero.

The horses already nervous, flung frantic weights into the traces. The stage lurched forward. Alma, one foot on the step and handicapped by the ankle she had twisted earlier, was swept off balance, fell heavily, reaching with one freed hand for support. The shock of her fall jarred Julie from her other arm.

The child was thrown under the stage as she fell. The "heavy back wheel foiled toward her body...."

CHAPTER 3
"THAT'S SENSE."

FLINT MADDOX pulled his mount up into a rearing halt and cursed. "Those skunks have hurt that kid!" he exclaimed.

15

The others pulled up also, following his backward glance. Flint wheeled his horse. "We've got to go back," he said grimly.

"Easy, Flint!" Charlie Parr warned. "Those buzzards have got their guns back. They'll go to shootin' if we ride back there."

"It's our fault if the kid's hurt," Flint said savagely. "We got to go back."

Doc Grimson nodded. "Flint's right," he agreed briefly. "But let's try to make them understand that we're coming on a peaceable mission this time. No use having any killing if we can get out of it."

"Shucks, Doc," Lockjaw Johnson grumbled. "What's the use of bein' so mealy-mouthed. That there ain't nothin' but a sheriff. If the pole-cat wants to lean on a bullet, why let him!"

But Flint Maddox had scarcely listened to the end of Lockjaw's speech. He set spurs to his mount and broke for the stage at a gallop. Lance Clayton followed, the others thundering behind him.

Lance leaned over the neck of his horse and spoke to him in a low, urgent voice. "Fog it, boy! Pass him!" he breathed.

He wanted to reach the stage ahead of Flint for two reasons. One was that, in case trouble started, he was a better shot with a six-gun than Flint. The other lay in his understanding of Flint's character. Flint was excited, beside himself at the thought that a child had been hurt and he would be more likely to start trouble than to try to avoid it.

Flint had once had children of his own, and a wife he had worshipped. All had been lost in an incendiary fire—a fire which, Flint had reason to believe, had been instigated by a range-hog who wished to grab onto Flint's spread. Flint had killed the stockman and his foreman in a saloon gun-fight and then fled the town two jumps in the lead of a crooked sheriff who wanted to pin a charge of murder on him. Bitterly, Flint had taken the Owlhoot Trail, and eventually had thrown in with Doc Grimson and Charlie Parr and Lockjaw Johnson, finding their peculiar brand of outlawry congenial to him.

Grizzled, mustached Charlie Parr had been a member of Boot Hill Kennedy's gang, and had killed that famous ruffian and murderer in a fight after Charlie objected to Kennedy's promiscuous shooting of innocent people, whose only offense had been to be in the way when a robbery was being pulled off. After Boot Hill's demise, Charlie had taken over the leadership, but his private code of honesty and decency had made him unpopular with that hard-bitten crew, and he had left them, followed by the faithful Lockjaw Johnson. Lockjaw hadn't understood the fine points of the dispute very well, but Lockjaw had the kind of loyalty that didn't need to understand. "Charlie, right or wrong" had been his motto, and it still was.

Of these men, Doc Grimson was the only one to whom any mystery attached. Doc had never told even his partners why he, a man of culture and an apparently first-rate physician, had come West to live outside the law. He never spoke of the past, not even of his past life in the West. They knew him only for what he was when they had met—a fast and deadly hand with a gun, a brilliant, though quixotic leader, and the best of partners.

These four were made to order for Lance Clayton, who had left his home town with a posse behind him merely because a lady had confided her misfortunes to him. Lance had stuck up a saloon, turned the proceeds over to the unhappy enchantress (who later repudiated him publicly and privately) and shaken the dust of that place from the heels of a providentially fast horse.

Together, the quintette ranged from the badlands of Montana to the hills of Chihuahua, acquiring a reputation which proved bewildering both to those who remained within the law and those who rode outside it. For they were as likely to fall upon and despoil the riders of the Owlhoot Trail as they were to turn to and risk their lives in the cause of the underdog.

UNDER LANCE'S urging the sorrel flashed into a magnificent burst of speed, drew level with Flint's horse, then began to draw away from him, stride by stride. He was not able to see exactly what had happened. Apparently the little girl had been thrown under the stage and hurt. The passengers, the driver and guards were grouped around her and her mother. Now, however, Lance saw them turn and look toward him, warned, evidently, by the hoof-beats of the five racing horses.

He could see their startled expressions, see them spread out, hands going toward six-guns. Lance raised his right hand over his head in the Indian gesture of peace. He hoped the fools wouldn't begin to shoot. That would turn this unfortunate venture of robbing the stage into a catastrophe.

His raised hand checked them for a moment; even Bogart appeared undecided as the stallion slid to stop before them.

"Don't go for your guns," Lance called sharply. "We're only aimin' to see what happened to the kid, and help her if we can."

Bogart's eyes were slitted as his hands hovered over his Colts. The others pulled up at Lance's side, and Doc Grimson slipped out of his saddle.

He landed standing at the head of a ground-tied horse, weight on his toes, legs spread a little, hands hanging, quiet and somehow all the more dangerous, near the butts of the two Colts in the worn black holsters which rode low on his thighs.

"You'd be a fool to start anything," he said crisply to Bogart. "You may be good with a gun, but your partners won't be good enough. You'd lose. What about a truce? We do anything we can for the kid, then we get a chance to ride as far away as we were before—without any trouble."

"What makes you think you can do anything for the kid?" Bogart sneered, his hot eyes searching Doc Grimson's face above the bandanna.

One of the guards took that moment to remember his oath. Lance guessed that the guard figured that the attention of the five long-riders would be all taken up with Bogart. Out of the corner of his eye Lance could see the man's hand tighten on the rifle. Lance didn't have time to say anything to stop the rash play for the guard moved too fast. The muzzle of his rifle swung sharply and leveled hip-high at Doc Grimson.

It leveled but that was all. Three Colts roared in a triple report that was like a single explosion.

"Hold it!" Doc Grimson said sharply as smoke curled up from the muzzles of Doc's and Charlie's revolvers. For Bogart's guns were in his hands, too.

Lance's eyes widened a little with respect as he realized the speed of the sheriff's draw. It wasn't possible to judge whether Bogart was as fast with a gun as they were, because they had had the advantage of surprise. The guard had been standing behind the sheriff, so the latter could not have realized what was coming. But if Bogart's draw had not been as fast as theirs, it had been too near it for comfort.

Bogart and Doc Grimson were confronting each other now, the sheriff's Colts trained on Doc's stomach, and Doc's held with equal steadiness on Bogart.

"Put up your guns," Doc commanded curtly, "unless you want to start a slaughter like that fool tried to do." He jerked his head toward the guard.

The guard's body had crumpled to the ground. Lance could see the red spurting under his shirt on the right side. He judged that the man was not mortally hurt. Like himself, the others had shot to disable, and not to kill.

Bogart hesitated.

"You can't win," Doc told him. "Nobody in your crowd has got his irons out but you." It was true. The other passengers had not tried to draw, but stood open-mouthed, like men who were a little stunned at seeing speed such as they had scarcely dreamed of.

Bogart's Colts lowered, dropped to their holsters, slid in. "That's sense," Doc approved.

The sheriff's eyes were small black hells of hatred and fury. "My deal's comin'," he ground out, "and then—God help you!"

Doc said to Charlie: "You and the others herd this crowd up toward the horses to give the little girl some air while I look at her. Keep your guns on them, just so nobody else gets optimistic."

Lance knew he wanted them out of the way, so that nobody would realize, from the expertness of his examination, that he was a doctor. He let the others take care of the passengers, himself going to help Doc. Then he saw that Flint had had the same idea. He should have thought of that—naturally, Flint wouldn't be kept away from the little girl. Charlie and Lockjaw could handle that crew, they were plenty bluffed already.

The young mother of the child was staring at them with eyes in which grief and terror mingled with surprise and bewilderment. The little girl in her arms appeared to he unconscious.

Doc Grimson took the child from her and laid her carefully on the ground. His gray eyes were serious now—intent, absorbed. His supple-fingered hands moved swiftly, baring the child's body, exploring the delicate, bruised abdomen over which the wheel of the stage had evidently passed. Flint stood looking on silently, his hands clenched into fists.

"No bones broken." Doc's voice was crisp, sure—a physician's voice, unmistakably. The woman at any rate would know that he was a doctor. In fact, she already knew a good deal too much. It was lucky that Flint had had his back turned to the others when the kid had unmasked him. Lance wondered if this woman—she looked little more than a girl—would talk. Somehow, he thought she would not. In her distress, her overwhelming anxiety about the little girl, she looked sweet and essentially good, as well as pretty.

Still, you never could tell. Women were unreliable and chancy, as he knew to his sorrow. If she held them responsible for the youngster's getting hurt…. If he had known that she was the wife of John Blake, town marshal, he would have been more worried.

Doc Grimson was saying: "It's impossible to tell whether or not there are internal injuries. You must get her to a doctor at once. There's a fairly good man in Tarpaulin, isn't there?"

"Yes. Dr. Ed Downer—he—he's our family doctor—everybody's."

"Then don't worry. It may be only a bad bruise. But get her to him as quickly as possible."

"Why—why is she unconscious?"

"Abdominal shock. There's no head injury. Don't worry now; your physician will be able to pull her through anything which may develop."

With Flint's help he lifted her into the coach. Lance saw Flint reach out a hard hand which was somehow wonderfully gentle on the tossed mop of curls over the pallid, exquisite face.

CHAPTER 4
MAVERICKS RIDE!

B Y TWO o'clock that afternoon the stage had reached Tarpaulin and news of the hold-up raced through the town like fire through a stand of dry alfalfa. Bogart's unattackable stage successfully robbed, with the sheriff himself a passenger and the principal loser! That was news! Details tumbled from excited lips, rebounding from ear to tongue and back again, losing nothing in the telling. Contradictory reports pursued one another from bar to bar. Bogart had been taken for ten thousand dollars. Twenty. He had not lost anything, the robbers having been fooled by an empty wallet. The fat man had risked death to save Marshal Blake's wife from insult; he had been shot by the hold-up men because he tried to conceal his money. Mrs. Blake's little girl had been killed; was gravely wounded, accidentally shot when the heroic guards resisted the robbers. She had been run over by the stage; by one of the highwayman's horses.

So great was the excitement that the garbled stories penetrated even to the back room of Chihuahua Sam's obscure saloon, where a gambler known as Friendly Joe Tarbell talked in low tones to a half-breed Apache called Moccasin Pete. Before their whispered conference was over, money passed from the gambler's hand to the breed's dirty palm and Joe Tarbell permitted a half-smile of satisfaction to break the poker mask of his features. A waiter, as he went out, told him the news, and Tarbell was so interested that he forgot to wonder at the waiter's being so near the inner door. There were five of the bandits? Friendly Joe knew of a certain five men who were not too careful in their respect for the law. His heart lightened still further within him.

By ten minutes past two, Alma Blake had learned that Dr. Ed Downer had been called out of town on an urgent case and would not be back until the next day. She took her little girl home in a neighbor's buckboard, her eyes wide with sudden fear.

By two-thirty Sheriff Bogart had gathered a posse and prepared to take the trail after the robbers. Joe Tarbell saw him at
the head of the posse and smiled a little, grimly. As he watched,
one of Bogart's henchmen hurried up and spoke to him in low,
urgent tones. The sheriff's expression changed a little, then he
leaned down and spoke hurriedly, his eyes narrowed and the
set of his mouth cruel. The messenger nodded and backed away
as the group of horsemen, at Bogart's signal, swept past him.

An hour later, the body of a half-breed known as Moccasin
Pete was found dead in a back alley not far from Chihuahua
Sam's saloon. A knife had been slipped into his ribs from behind.
Nobody paid much attention to that. He was nothing but
another breed.

Toward sunset, Sheriff Bogart and his posse were still out
when five men rode into Tarpaulin and inquired their way to
the house of Friendly Joe Tarbell. The citizen to whom they
addressed themselves eyed them curiously, then stiffened a little,
as though an unpleasant thought had occurred to him. He told
them, however, that Joe Tarbell lived in a one-room shack on
the edge of town and gave them directions for finding it.

When he had gone, Charlie Parr said sourly: "That feller was
suspicious, just because there are five of us. I told you we ought
to have waited until dark. If we run into that woman who saw
Flint's face, we're cooked."

Doc Grimson nodded gloomily. "I reckon you're right," he
agreed. And then after a moment: "Sorry, Charlie."

Charlie Parr looked suddenly abashed. "Hell, Doc," he said

uncomfortably. "It don't matter. I know you was worried about this old pardner of yours."

Lance Clayton said cheerfully: "Let 'em suspect. They can't prove anything. And us riding into town openly this way may do more to throw 'em off the track than anything else would."

"I don't believe she'd say anything if she did see me," Flint Maddox said, looking stubborn.

"Who wouldn't say anything?" Lockjaw asked.

"The woman."

"What woman?"

Charlie Parr raised resigned eyes to heaven, made strangled sounds of prayer and supplication. Then, after a moment he said: "Listen, Lockjaw—try to throw your mind way back to noon today. Do you remember that we held up a stage—with a lady on it?"

Lockjaw said: "Oh!"

"Oh? Oh, what?"

Lockjaw looked a little bewildered. "Sure, I remember, Charlie," he said, placatingly. "I didn't know you was talkin' about *her*."

DOC GRIMSON cut in diplomatically: "Maybe we'll be able to turn over this *dinero* to Friendly Joe and then hit the breeze."

"I don't think so," Lance said. "His letter sounded like he needed plenty of help. Besides, what can Bogart do? We'll just face him down—that's all."

"If his health can't do without a little shootin'," Flint put in savagely, "I'll sure be glad to oblige him."

Lance knew he was thinking of the little girl who had been hurt because Bogart lost his head. It was because of her, even more than to help Joe Tarbell, that Flint had insisted on riding into Tarpaulin without waiting for the cover of darkness. He would not be easy until he found out that she was all right.

Underneath his cheerful exterior, Lance was feeling sober enough. He had a hunch they were running into a lot of trouble. He thought of Flint's conviction that the little girl's mother wouldn't betray him and remembered the lady for whom he, Lance, had stepped outside the law. You couldn't count on women. By now, probably, this one was blaming them for her little girl's accident and wanting to see them all strung up.

"This must be the place," Doc Grimson said, halting before a small frame shack, old and dilapidated.

"It don't look so prosperous," Charlie Parr commented, eyeing it skeptically.

"I reckon Joe's been living plenty simple," Doc Grimson said softly, "putting everything aside for that kid of his and the spread he's looking to buy her. He's loco about her."

He dismounted and knocked at the closed door. "Hey, you ornery, stove-up tinhorn," he called out cheerfully. "Show your ugly mug—you've got visitors."

There was no answer. "Out somewhere, I guess," Doc said, his face falling a little.

"Maybe this ain't the right shack," Charlie suggested, but he dismounted nevertheless.

Lance sucked in his breath suddenly. From his position he could see the side of the house. Where the crudely-carpentered outer wall met the flooring something dark showed. As his eye fell on it, that something collected itself into a globule, hung poised an instant, and then dropped softly into the dust.

Lance flung himself from his horse. "Open the door, Doc," he said in a voice suddenly harsh.

Doc Grimson shot him a quick glance, then, as though his question had been answered, lifted the latch of the door. It gave easily. Without hesitation, he stepped in, but froze in his tracks after one step. The others, pressing in beside him, did likewise.

Friendly Joe Tarbell lay face downward on the floor. A crimson pool circled his body and ran off in rivulets to the side wall. But it did not need that to tell them that there was no need to rush to his aid. The rigid posture of his body was more eloquent still. Joe Tarbell was dead.

Doc Grimson stared at him, his eyes bitter and the muscles of his jaws standing out in corrugated ridges. The others likewise were silent, hard-eyed.

After a long moment, Doc went to the body, turned it over gently. The gambler's jugular vein had been cut.

He said softly, as though thinking aloud: "No sign of a fight, but his gun is out of his holster."

Charlie Parr motioned toward an open window at the other side. "Looks like the knife was thrown," he said grimly.

But Doc Grimson was not listening. His eyes were fixed on some marks on the floor near the dead man's right hand. The others followed the direction of his gaze. Dying, Joe Tarbell had dipped his finger in his own blood and written, "Bank—bog."

The "g" of the last word was only partly finished. It trailed off, shakily, as though the dying man's strength had failed.

LANCE CLAYTON whistled. "Bogart!" he exclaimed softly.

Charlie Parr's white mustache bristled with perplexity. "Funny," he commented, finally, "Bogart couldn't have killed him. He was leadin' that posse we slipped this afternoon."

"And why 'bank?'" Flint Maddox asked.

"Exactly!" Doc Grimson raised eyes in which the beginnings of a strange understanding mingled with bitterness. "Why 'bank?'"

"Funny," Charlie repeated. "Why didn't he write the name of the man who threw the knife. He must have got a look at him, because he had time to pull his hawgleg either just before or just after the knife hit him."

"You don't think he meant that Bogart had him killed, Doc?" Lance Clayton asked.

Doc Grimson eyed him queerly. "I don't know," he said.

He got to his feet with a sudden decisive movement.

"Listen, boys," he said, "I'm askin' you a favor. The job we came to do here is done. We've got the money to make the last payment on that spread for Joe's kid. I'll see that she's taken care of. There isn't any more we can do. I want you boys to pull out."

"You mean you're lettin' this murder go by?" asked Charlie Parr sardonically.

Doc's eyes blazed. "No!" he snapped. "I'll let it go when the skunk who killed him is dead—not before!"

"Well—?" asked Lance softly.

Doc answered, mastered the flare of passion which had made his voice shake. "We're in a tight here. The longer we stay, the worse it will get. We've got the law against us and back of that law we've got a sidewinder who won't stop at anything. Bogart owns this county. If we walk back into that town tonight, we walk into a nest of rattle-snakes. Until I can get something on Bogart, our lives are in danger every minute. Joe was my friend. His murder is my private affair. I want you to pull out—hit the trail! You can't do any good here. If I need you, I'll send for you."

"While you stay and get yourself dry-gulched, for nosin' around—like Joe did!" commented Lance scornfully. "What do you take us for, Doc? I'm stickin'!"

Charlie Parr laughed shortly. "Don't be a fool, Doc," he said. "We're all stickin'!"

"Check!" Flint rasped.

Lockjaw said contemptuously. "Since when have we been runnin' from tin-stars?"

For a second they stared at one another, faces grim, across the body of the dead man. The room was so silent that they could hear the faint drip-drip of the slow, dark tide which still ran under the side wall to fall onto the ground outside.

Doc's eyes were fixed thoughtfully on Flint, and Lance guessed that he was thinking that he was the weak spot. Without the possibility of identifying him, they might bluff it out. Then he saw Doc's features relax. "Well—I don't know but that I'm glad," he said at last, softly.

Flint had caught his look. "I tell you she won't talk," he said stubbornly.

Lance saw Charlie Parr turn his eyes away to hide the cynical doubt in them. He said easily: "Maybe we won't run into her."

"I think there's blood on the moon," said Doc grimly. "Maybe it's ours. But let's go."

"What's the play, Doc?"

Doc Grimson shrugged. "Circulate around and keep our ears open. I hear the Nugget's the big saloon here. Let's start there." TEN MINUTES later they were lined up at the bar. The stage stick-up was still the talk of the town. Bogart and the posse had not been heard from, but men repeated the details they already knew with undiminished gusto, and speculation as to the eventual fate of the robbers was free and large.

"They got a good start," Lance heard one man argue. "If they've got sense, they're foggin' it for the Border now. They may get away."

His companion shook his head. "Bogart's a hound on the trail," he said confidently. "Got his trainin' from the Apaches. I wouldn't like to be in the boots of any jasper he's after."

"What about the little girl?" Flint asked the bartender.

"Bad, I reckon," was the indifferent response. "She ain't dead yet." He was a pasty-faced man, with a cast in one eye and a slick lock of hair plastered low on a villainous forehead.

Lockjaw Johnson eyed him with disfavor. "It ain't no skin off your mug, what happens to a little kid, is it?" he asked disagreeably.

The bartender looked at him malevolently but his gaze fell

before Lockjaw's stony stare. "It wasn't me that hurt her," he muttered sullenly.

A dusty, sweat-stained man came in the saloon door and walked rapidly toward the bar. "Whisky, Ike," he commanded. He looked self-important.

"Wasn't you with the posse?" the bartender asked eagerly, as he reached for a bottle and glass. "Is there any news?"

"Is there any news?" the newcomer repeated, raising his voice a little. "No, there's not any news—except that we've got the robbers!"

The bar-room was suddenly silent, necks craning in his direction.

"You snagged 'em, did you?" exclaimed the man who had bragged of Bogart's ability on a trail. "I said Bogart would have 'em behind bars before nightfall!"

"They ain't behind the bars yet," the newcomer said. "But they're the same as." He paused, enjoying the sensation he was creating, A dozen voices plied him with excited questions.

"Them fellers was pretty smart," he said, taking his time, "but they made a big mistake. I'll tell you how it was. They thought they had throwed us off the trail—and they had! Oh, they're smart, all right! Even Bogart was off scent. But what do them jaspers do? Why, they get 'em a change of horses an' take a roundabout trail—where? *Right square into this town!*

"They thought nobody would think of their doin' that, I guess," he went on, "but they didn't figure on Bogart's bein' a ridin' fool. When he lost their trail he started cuttin' wide for sign. Before long he come on the tracks of five horses, leadin'

31

from Blood Mountain. Five of 'em, see? The tracks led straight here. They was different tracks from the ones we followed but there ain't no doubt that those are the men."

Charlie Parr looked at him from under lazy lids. "How do you expect to prove it?" he asked lazily.

"They're bringin' Marshal Blake's wife in right now. She saw one of 'em—her kid pulled his mask off. She'll be able to identify 'em."

"Ah!" the crowd breathed, tensing. Many turned instinctively toward the door, as though they expected dramatic action from that direction at any moment. A few, who had noticed the five strangers who had strolled in a few minutes before, shot them curious, cautious glances. But the five, who leaned now with their backs to the bar in casual postures, appeared if anything less excited than any one else.

"They're makin' a search for 'em right now," the posseman went on. The bartender was frowning and making furtive signs at him, but he was enjoying his importance too much to heed them. "We've got the town surrounded so's they can't get out, an'—"

He broke off. A man had come in at the saloon door. He was a thin man, so blond as to be almost albino, and he wore a badge on his shirt. A single gunbelt let a pair of worn holsters hang, unstrapped, at his hips. These holsters were cut off at the bottoms, so that the blued barrels of his Colts showed naked—"halfbreed" holsters, from which a man could shoot without drawing his guns.

HE STOOD with his legs apart and his thumbs in his belt,

scanning the room with cold, almost colorless eyes. His glance had something of the effect of a blight. As men realized his presence, they fell silent, shifted uneasily on their feet.

"Doin' some talkin', Potter?" he asked at last, ominously. His voice was as cold as his eyes. The words left his lips with a curious, snake-like slither.

The posseman swallowed hard. "Uh—just stopped in for a little drink, Marshal," he muttered. "Uh—cut the dust. Goin' right out."

He sidled hastily toward the door, gained it, and popped out, with the effect of a scurrying rabbit.

The crowd which had surrounded him broke up into groups, separating, as though by common accord. The thin man continued to scan the room, his eyes pausing from time to time in the appraisal of someone who, it seemed probable, was a stranger to him. Four of the five men at the bar bore his scrutiny carelessly. The fifth glared back at him with growing belligerence.

All five knew that this must be John Blake, husband of the woman who had been on the stage and reputed to be one of the coldest-blooded killers since Buckskin Frank Leslie. They had heard of him when they investigated Bogart in Jackson Corners. He was, it was said, one of the sheriff's henchmen but considered even more dangerous than his chief. Men said that he never lost his head, never took an unnecessary chance, and was dazzlingly fast with a gun.

For a second he coldly returned Lockjaw Johnson's belligerent stare. Then he turned and looked at a man who stood at his shoulder. The man nodded almost imperceptibly and, at a gesture from Blake, went out. The marshal himself strolled to the other end of the bar and took up a position around the bend.

Lance Clayton let out his breath with a soft little hiss. "You'll get yourself killed that way some day, Lockjaw," he said gloomily. "You're not exactly lightnin' on the draw, you know."

"Hell," Lockjaw bragged complacently. "I been shot lots of times. These here now fast gunmen," he amplified, "they fan a quick shot through you most anywhere, irregardless. If you have any luck, you get a chance to get one shot in, anyway. Me, I don't need but one chance—I place my shots." He looked extremely well satisfied with himself.

Lance looked at his dumb, horse-long face resignedly. No use arguing with him. He was right about one thing anyway— if Lockjaw ever got a chance to place a shot, it would be just too bad for somebody.

"What do you think, Doc?" Charlie Parr lipped softly but with the casual air of a man commenting on the weather. "Think we better make a break for it?"

Doc shook his head. "No," he said coolly. "We'd never get to our horses. This is just about as good a place to face it out as any."

Two men came in and joined the marshal at the bar. They packed two guns each, worn low.

A moment later two more drifted in and, at a nod from the marshal, took seats at a corner table. They also bore the obvious brand of the hired gun-fighter.

A man about thirty years old, with clear-cut, open features

and candid eyes, who was sitting at a table by himself, glanced at the two latest comers and frowned involuntarily. Then his eyes sought the five men at the bar, searching their countenances in anxious, questioning appraisal.

The saloon doors swung back again, gustily this time, to admit Sheriff Ben Bogart and two of his deputies.

The man's very physical presence was like the blow of a fist. It struck the room into silence, just as Blake's reptilian coldness had, a few moments before, fascinated it into silence. Looking at the two now, it was possible to see without difficulty why Bogart was the master.

His blazing gaze swept the room, came to rest on the five men lined up at the bar, passed on with a question to Blake. "Are those the men?" he snapped.

The town marshal, followed by his gunmen, moved out a little from the bend of the bar. "Yeah," he answered, his eyes on the five. "Those are the ones."

The two gunmen who had taken a seat at one of the tables got up and slouched over to stand at the sheriff's side.

"Come over here, you men," Bogart said sternly, "and stand in front of me."

For the space of a heart beat no one moved. After that, the room was full of movement, but it was not the movement of the five against the bar—it was the movement of other men who had seen that this five did not intend to obey, who had sensed from their postures and the granite coldness of their gaze that a word, a wrong gesture, would be enough to set off a sudden hell of gun-fire and flailing lead. Five against eight;

thirteen Colts belching thunder and retching death. No one wanted to be in the way of that storm when it broke.

"Well," Blake snapped up. "Step up! You aren't afraid, are you?"

"We can hear you from here," Doc Grimson said, ominously quiet, "and we don't like your tone any. Better call your play—whatever it is."

Bogart's eyes flared anger, but he held himself in. "I think I've heard that voice before," he rasped. "We'll see." He turned to the marshal. "All right, Blake," he said.

Blake crossed to the entrance doors. His two companions remained where they were. In that position they would be able to bring something like a flanking fire to bear on the five if trouble started.

Blake said: "Come in, Alma."

In response, Alma Blake stepped into the saloon. Her face was pale and drawn, her hands, held rigidly at her sides, were clenched, nervous.

"Ever see any of those men before?"

Her eyes fell first on Flint Maddox and her pallor increased. They flinched away, sought, as though automatically, the faces of the other four. She looked at each one carefully, thoroughly.

"Well?" Bogart questioned impatiently.

The woman's eyes went back to Flint Maddox. Her lips tightened a little. She took a long breath. Then she said in a clear, firm voice: "No; I've never seen any of these men before."

CHAPTER 5
KILLERS' TRACKS

S ILENCE. NONE of the men before her changed expression. None of the men at her side moved or spoke. She turned to look at the sheriff. His eyes were fixed on her in a kind of profound astonishment. His face had gone several shades paler, so that the dark blaze of his eyes was accentuated.

Her husband's look was coldly disbelieving, angry.

"One flush that you didn't fill, Sheriff," Doc Grimson said evenly. Bogart glared at him, his hand twitching a little.

"Ma'am," Flint Maddox addressed her earnestly. "I hear your little girl was hurt this afternoon. I hope she's all right."

"I—I'm terribly afraid—she seems to be hurt so badly."

Flint looked as though somebody had struck him. He half-opened his mouth to speak, then closed it again.

"The doctor…." Alma went on. Her husband interrupted coldly: "That's enough! We'll have no more palaver."

Flint Maddox showed a face like sudden granite, eyes narrowed, hard. Lance said, with calculated, intolerable insolence: "Don't interrupt a lady and a gentleman when they're talkin', you."

Alma said hastily: "I must go now." She turned and went to the door. Her husband stood rigid; his eyes glittered coldly, like those of a snake about to strike, as Alma Blake went out, into the clear late-afternoon light.

When she was gone, Ben Bogart spoke. "Maybe you hombres will explain where you were at noon today," he said slowly.

"Maybe is exactly the right word, Bogart," Doc Grimson said gently. "Maybe we will—but most likely we won't."

"I suppose you know that five men—*five*, you understand—held up the stage today. You got into town about an hour ago, I've been told. You came from Blood Mountain. I followed the tracks of your horses in. The five men who robbed the stage disappeared on Blood Mountain. *And you look to me like those men.*"

Charlie Parr said dryly: "There ain't no magic in the number five, as I've heard of. Seven, yes. But five—no. If you're goin' in for fortune-tellin', Bogart, you'd better pick another number."

"And just how come us to look like those men?" asked Lance Clayton. "Did you see their faces?"

"And about that Blood Mountain," said Doc Grimson. "That won't wash, Bogart. I'll lay you odds that I can pick you five strangers in town tonight, all of whom came in less than an hour ago, and none of whom will tell you where they were this afternoon, unless you ask them a good deal more politely than you did us. If your stage robbers had the nerve to come into town tonight, it's a good bet that they had sense enough to come in separately. No—it won't do. I'm afraid you'll have to do a little more work than this to earn your pay, Mister Sheriff."

Bogart's face had grown a shade whiter and the set of his jaw a shade deadlier with each succeeding speech.

"You're right," he said now, his eyes narrowed. "I can't prove anything against you with the evidence I've got now. But I can tell you this—you're not welcome here. I know of you, know your reputation. You've split things wide open up and down the country for a long time—mostly without leaving any actual evidence behind you. You're supposed to be bad medicine, and you get-away with a lot on bluff. But you've come to the wrong town. I'm callin' you, and I'm callin' plenty. Fork your horses and get out of this county and stay out of it. If you don't, I'll make it my business to see that you don't ever leave it. And that goes as it lays."

"You're running too high a blaze, Bogart," Doc Grimson snapped. "We're not figuring to leave town tomorrow, or any other day, until it suits us to."

"And *that* goes as it lays," Charlie Parr added dryly.

"So if you're honin' to do any shooting," Flint Maddox snarled, "this is just as good a time as any. You won't find it so easy as running over children."

"Sure! Cut the palaver and jerk 'em," Lockjaw lipped belligerently. "This ain't no prayer meeting."

Lance Clayton said nothing. He simply laughed. And there was something at once contemptuous and joyous in his laughter.

A gasp ran around the room. Nobody had ever talked to Ben Bogart like that before. Nobody had ever dreamed that anybody would. There wasn't a man in the room who didn't assume that these hard-eyed strangers had signed their own death-warrants. But there was admiration in the eyes of the men who backed closer against the walls to be clear of flying lead.

The sheriff had gone rigid. His hands hovered, limp and deadly supple over the butts of his six-guns. John Blake looked more venomous than ever. The other six shifted to the gun-fighter's position, legs spread, weight balanced lightly on the toes.

For a long time; for an endless time—for the time it might take for a man's heart to beat twice, slowly—the silence held. So long that men had time to wonder if Sheriff Ben Bogart was not being bluffed.

Then a new voice cracked across the room. "Take your hand off that knife, you Mexican skunk!"

STARTLED EYES shifted to the speaker, saw a man of about thirty, with open, clear-cut features and blazing eyes. He had a six-gun in his hand. It was pointed toward the partition at the bend of the bar where a Mexican stood suddenly frozen, a snarl on his lips.

"Jud Pearson!" somebody breathed in astonishment.

"Get your hands up, Greaser—or I'll blow your yellow guts out."

Still snarling like a cornered bob-cat, the Mexican raised his hands above his head.

Ben Bogart's eyes blazed fury. "What's all this about?" he demanded threateningly.

The man at the table said: "Bogart, I've tried to play along with you—like a lot of other people—because I knew you could make me trouble in this county. But when a white man gets to hiring Mex knife-throwers it's more than a man can stand. I'm warnin' you, if trouble starts, I'm fannin' my gun on the side of these other men. You been bulldozin' this county for too long. I'm plumb ashamed that it had to take five strangers to call you on it."

Doc Grimson had been staring, like a man transfixed. Now his voice crackled in sudden, searing anger. "A knife-thrower, huh? Bogart, what you know about the death of Friendly Joe Tarbell?"

The sheriff's face was suddenly an expressionless mask. "I didn't know Tarbell was dead," he said evenly.

"I think you're lying, Bogart," Doc Grimson blazed. "I think you know plenty about it. By God, will you go for your gun now—or will you wait until I put a rope around your neck? One way or the other, I'm goin' to get you."

A dusty, excited rider plunged in at the door. His glance fell at once on the sheriff and not realizing the situation he was breaking into, he went to him without hesitation. "I've got news, Sheriff," he said in a low voice.

Bogart hesitated, then walked aside with him. When, a moment later, he came back to his place, his eyes were blazing with venomous triumph.

"So you're going to get me, are you?" he snapped. "Well, I don't think you are, my four-flushing friend. This is enough talk for now. If you got guts enough to stay in town until tomorrow, we'll see who gets who."

He turned on his heel and went out. Blake and the others followed him, after a moment of dazed hesitation. Behind them they left in the Nugget Saloon a motionless panorama of slack jaws and astonished eyes.

DOC GRIMSON held out his hand to Jud Pearson. "I'm thankin' you, amigo," he said warmly. "If that Mexican had thrown his knife, it would have done more than just get one of us. It would have attracted our attention long enough to let that crowd get the jump on us. I think you've saved all our lives."

The others added their hand-grips to Doc's, took seats at Pearson's table.

"It's for me to thank you," Pearson told them. "You've done a lot for this county tonight. You've given a lot of us hope and courage. And we needed it bad."

"You think maybe folks are gittin' a mite tired of this Bogart?" Charlie Parr asked.

"Hell!" exclaimed Pearson. "This county would celebrate for a week if anybody got rid of that wolf. But nobody's got the guts to go after him. He's too strong. Folks that get rambunctious have a habit of acquirin' hard luck. It ain't healthy."

"So that's why you strung in with us tonight!" Lance smiled at him. "I couldn't just figure it."

"Maybe that wasn't all the reason," Pearson said calmly. "Maybe I had another. Jim Wallace, who drives the stage, is a good friend of mine. I got the straight of the stick-up from him. I heard that the robbers hadn't robbed anybody but a skunk. I heard that they shot to disable when most men would have shot to kill. And I heard the chance they took in comin' back when Alma Blake's little girl was hurt. Maybe I thought that if you was bein' accused of bein' those fellers you was worth givin' a hand to. I—I think a lot of—of that little kid," he ended, flushing a little.

Doc Grimson appeared to be only half-listening. He looked moody, abstracted. He asked, with apparent irrelevance. "If

Bogart had something to hide, where do you think he'd hide it?"

Pearson smiled. "In a place that you and I couldn't get into," he replied grimly.

"You mean by that that you don't know?"

"I mean by that that I do know. Bogart's got a private vault in the bank. Had workmen come in clear from Denver to build it for him. Everybody knows that, but he's the only one on earth who knows the combination. And it would need a ton of dynamite to blast that vault loose. Beside it, the regular vault of the bank is nothing but a tin can."

Doc Grimson's eyes blazed. "So!" he said softly.

He exchanged significant glances with the others.

"That's it!" Lance said triumphantly. He, like the others, was remembering a scrawl written in blood—a scrawl which read, "Bank—Bog."

Pearson looked bewildered, then he asked quickly, incredulously: "You don't mean you're going to try to rob that bank?"

Doc Grimson looked at Charlie Parr, who nodded. "I reckon we may as well lay our cards on the table with you, Pearson," he said, lowering his voice. Then, briefly, he recounted what had happened to Friendly Joe. "I figured right away that Joe knew who killed him—it was likely that Mex you cut down on—but he knew also that Bogart was the man who had hired him to do it. Joe had something on Bogart—and the proof of that something must be in the bank. And Joe, being a clear-headed gent, and knowing that he didn't have much time or strength, went right after the big casino. He wanted to tell us that we could get Bogart through the bank somehow. If he had lived long enough he might have put the Mexican's name down, too. But that wasn't the important thing, and he didn't live to finish.

"Now that you've told us about Bogart's private vault, that makes me feel all the more certain. Anyway, that's where we've got to strike—if for no other reason than that there's no other angle to go after. I don't know what they've run onto out there on Blood Mountain. If they've lucked onto our extra horses, then there's a chance that they'll find our cache and plenty of identifiable property that belongs to us. They'll also find tracks of both sets of horses leading in and out of that area. And all that will be proof enough. We'll not only have Bogart against us then, we'll have the law and the town down on us. We'll have to high-tail it out of here. That crowds us, you see. We've only got until tomorrow morning, at best. We've got to strike at Bogart tonight—and that bank vault's the only way I see."

LOCKJAW HAD been following this explanation with growing excitement. Now he exclaimed delightedly. "That's right! And if we don't get into the private vault, we'll clean out the big one, anyway. Git somethin' for our trouble."

A couple of men playing a friendly game of seven-up at a nearby table, pricked up their ears, glanced out of the corner of their eyes, and then apparently became reabsorbed in their game.

Charlie Parr said in a low, savage voice, his face wreathed, in a pleasant smile: "That's right! Yell it all over town, you damn hammer-headed ignorant, bat-eared, thick-skulled slab of dried coyote bait!"

Lockjaw looked abashed. "Aw, nobody didn't hear nothin'," he said uneasily. He turned in his chair, saw the two at the other table, and started to get out of his chair. "If those buzzards are snoopin' around here, I'll show...."

"Sit down!" Charlie told him ferociously. Lockjaw subsided.

Pearson said: "You'll have to be careful in this town. Bogart's got spies everywhere. I don't know whether he pays 'em or whether they just run to him to lick his boots. Anyway, he hears everything that anybody ever says—and some they don't, I reckon."

Flint Maddox had listened to Doc's plan with approval. Now, however, he began to show signs of restlessness.

"I think I'll take a little *pasear* out to see how that kid's gettin' along," he said. "Where's their place, Pearson?"

"It's right out the road a piece. You want to go out? I'd like to go out myself."

"Better watch your step," Charlie Parr warned. "If Blake's out there, I wouldn't put it past him to gun you."

Lance said: "Lockjaw and I'll go, too. You won't need us until later, will you, Doc?"

Doc shook his head. "Plenty of time, yet."

The four went out, separating for the moment. Pearson had left his horse in front of the building; the mounts of the five were in the rear.

The light was still clear, though it was after sunset, and the three sauntered out the back door carelessly, but with eyes nonetheless alert. That was an automatic reaction to a strange and hostile town; but in this case, it was also lucky.

Lance caught it first—the glint of a rifle barrel from the shadowy window of a small adobe building some hundred feet behind the saloon. He yelled "Down" to the others and flung himself flat, just as the sharp, spatting crack rang out. Almost simultaneously, a six-gun spoke from the corner of a wooden shack nearby.

Lance had jerked his gun as he went down. Now he fanned two shots at the window which held the rifleman, saw him disappear, and flung a quick shot at the man with the Colt. The bullet struck the corner of the building sending up a shower of splinters, just as Flint's gun also spoke. The man gave a sharp cry of pain and ducked out of sight.

Lance flashed a glance to the rear to see if either of his companions were hurt. Both were flat on their bellies, Lockjaw hatless, his unfired Colt clutched in his hand, his eyes glaring.

There were several other buildings in front of them but none of them showed signs of danger. Lance found his feet like a cat and ran toward the adobe which had sheltered the rifleman, calling to Flint to cover the other danger-point.

As he passed the nearer, wooden shack, he shot a glance at the corner, but there was no one there. The man had evidently not been hurt badly enough to keep him from running.

The window, too, was empty as he came up to it, so he swerved and ran around to the rear. The back door was wide open, and Lance guessed that his bird had flown.

Together they searched the building, without finding evidence as to who had fired on them. It was an untenanted shack. Anybody might have gotten into it. They met Flint, who likewise had not gotten sight of his man. Together they walked back to the saloon to find Doc and Charlie at the door.

Charlie Parr said dryly, "You forgot your hat, Lockjaw," and handed the sombrero to its owner, displaying at the same time a neat round hole in the crown from front to center.

But Doc Grimson looked serious. "Watch yourselves, boys," he warned. "They may not be through yet."

CHAPTER 6
TWO-GUN MARSHAL

THE BLAKE ranch-house might have been small, but in the late evening light it looked wonderfully inviting to Flint Maddox. He pulled up some distance from it and sat gazing at it, oblivious of his companions.

The ranch-house sat in a grove of cottonwoods and willows by the side of a small creek. The creek formation, the three newcomers noted with the instinctive eyes of outdoor men for topography, was curious. The bank on the side opposite the house was much higher, and deeply undercut. So sharp was the cutaway, in fact, that it seemed a miracle that the whole bank did not collapse down into the creek. No doubt, the thick grass roots of the prairie on that side had so far prevented the crumbling of the upper edge, whereas the creek in flood had gradually eaten the bank beneath.

The sharp break from high level prairie on the far side to low level prairie on the rear could only be accounted for by some odd freak of geological strata. In any case, it gave the ranch-house an extraordinarily sheltered appearance, enhanced by the towering aspect of the trees on the far bank and increased further by the presence of an arroyo which cut into the creek from the near side, running apparently within two or three paces of the back door. The house was thus set in an angle, the creek to the side of the arroyo at the rear, and a pleasant stretch of trees, sparse brush and willow-tangle to the front. The corral and the other buildings were on the opposite of the creek, a well-made bridge leading to them.

Lance, watching Flint's face, knew what a strong appeal the place must be making to him. Funny sort of a fellow, Flint, he thought. He was apparently as crazy about cattle-ranching as some men are about liquor. It had been in his blood, heritage of his youth and his memories of his own ranch, and he never passed a good-looking spread without looking at it so wistfully as to make you believe that he would never be happy again until he got back to ranching. But that wasn't all of Flint. Lance knew that an even more potent liquor worked in the man's veins—the liquor of freedom and danger, the strong drink of change, of excitement, of faculties pitched high and full, of the constant acid testing which was the Outlaw Trail.

They had passed Blake in town as they came out, so now, after a moment, they rode straight for the house. Alma Blake came out to meet them.

"Oh!" she cried, "I'm so glad you came! I was praying you would."

She shot a somewhat shy look at Pearson and said: "I'm glad to see you, too, Jud."

Pearson introduced the others. "What can we do to help you, ma'am?" Flint asked directly.

"It's Julie," Alma told him quickly. "I'm so frightened about her. Something must be broken inside—she's so pale and she has so much trouble breathing. I thought if your friend…."

Flint's face tightened. "You bet he will, ma'am," he told her. "But didn't this sawbones here do nothin' for her?"

"Didn't you know?" Alma asked, with a catch in her voice. "But, of course—why should you? He was called away before we got here on a desperate case, forty miles from here. He won't be back before tomorrow. Nobody has seen her—nobody!"

Flint said something violent under his breath, He looked like a man guilty of murder. "What a fool I am!" he muttered. "If only I had gone to him first thing. But so much got happenin', ma'am…."

"Of course, it's not your fault," Alma said. "If only your friend can come quickly…." She broke off with a sob.

Lance saw that Flint was too torn for the moment to get his voice. Jud Pearson took an involuntary step toward the woman. "Don't—don't cry, Alma," he said. "It's sure to be all right." The look in his eyes was not to be mistaken. Lance guessed that he had loved this wife of another man for a long time—hopelessly.

Alma stifled her sobs and tried to smile at him through her tears. She held out her hand to him by way of thanks.

Flint got himself together. "He'll be here as fast as a bronc can carry him, ma'am," he promised and turned to mount.

"Who'll be here?" Blake's voice, cold-edged, asked from behind them.

Evidently he had left his horse on the road and walked softly up through the trees so as to remain unseen. For a moment there was silence. Then the woman turned to her husband, her manner apologetic, pleading.

"It's his friend—the doctor, John. I want him to come out and look at Julie. I'm so anxious about her. We can't wait on Dr. Ed because nobody can tell when he really will get here."

"You must be out of your head," Blake told her contemptuously. "No crooked pole-cat like that is goin' to doctor any child in this family."

He turned his sudden snake-like head on Pearson. "And when anybody has to hold my wife's hand, I'll do the holdin'," he snarled, unexpectedly. "You're happenin' around here too often. Git off my land, *now*—and if I catch you hangin' around here again, I'll let daylight through you."

"Oh!" Alma cried. It sounded as though he had struck her.

Pearson's face whitened, stiffened. He turned slowly toward Blake until he stood facing him squarely, his legs a little apart. The hand which hung near his holster twitched a little.

"*Your* land?" he asked scornfully. "You haven't got any land except what you got control of by trickin' a decent woman into marryin' you."

"Please! Please!" Alma begged, her voice almost frantic.

Pearson disregarded her. "You're a skunk, Blake," he went on. "You're skunk enough to mistreat one of the best women in this country. Everybody knows it. But not even I ever thought you'd be double-skunk enough to insult her the way you just have."

"Jud! Jud!" Alma cried, her voice frantic. "Don't! Can't you see what you're doing?"

Blake crouched a little, elbows bent, hands hovering near the two half-holsters on his hips. "Go for you...."

"No, you don't!" Flint's voice cut in sharp, imperative. "Wait a minute, Pearson! You spoke out of turn. This thing here that's lower than a pole-cat insulted my friend before he did his wife. I've got first call on him. By God, Blake, you'll draw first to me, or I'll cut you down from the side!"

LANCE CLAYTON had been watching the play with keen, comprehending eyes. He had seen Flint hesitate, struggle with himself, before he spoke, and his quick intelligence had leapt to the reason. Flint, like himself, had seen that Pearson loved Alma and had guessed that in her secret heart she might be ready to respond to him if she were not married. That gave Flint a more serious rival than the husband could be, and the perception, Lance saw at once, had hit Flint hard.

During all the course of the talk he had observed Flint's growing depression and, knowing him so thoroughly, had been able to guess at his thoughts. Here was a man, a neighboring rancher, whose hands were clean and who would some day, perhaps, make Alma Blake a good husband. Even if he, Flint, were able to get her away from him, what right would he have to do it—a man outside the law, to whom any one of a dozen offenses might some day come home; a man in danger of prison, even now, if Bogart's search should prove successful. And the conflict between desire and duty was difficult to resolve when one remembered that this woman might mean happiness to a man who had been long and brutally robbed of it.

Then, Blake had spoken and it had become immediately obvious that he would have to kill Pearson or be killed by him. It had forced Flint's decision. Lance knew that he interfered now, not only to save Alma's lover from possible death, but to save him also from something else. For if Pearson had the luck to kill Blake, he could scarcely, in decency, marry the woman who had been his wife. Either way it turned out, he lost. Flint meant to sacrifice himself in order that his rival might live—and live with clean hands.

"Old Flint!" Lance said softly under his breath. Aloud he said curtly. "I reckon not! I was with Doc before you were, Flint. This buzzard is *my* meat. You draw to me, Blake, or *I'll* get you from the side."

Blake's face was a snarl, cold with hate and growing cunning.

"You're all pretty anxious to collect my hide, aren't you?" he asked, shuttling narrowed eyes between the three.

"Speakin' for me, I'd say you were right," Flint ground out. "Fill your hand, you four-flusher. Lance, you keep out of this!"

Blake relaxed from his crouch, stood up straight, his manner cool again. "I reckon I'll wait until I can have something like a fair break," he said with slow insolence. "You yellow-backed scorpion," Flint told him scornfully. "You'll get a fair break. Lance, tell him you'll keep out of this."

Blake laughed coldly. "It wouldn't do any good," he said. "I'm not fool enough to trust him—or the others. This looks like a frame-up to me. Well, I'm not playin'—sabe? If you get me today, it'll be murder, with Mrs. Blake as a witness."

"Crawlin' out of it, are you?" Lance commented contemptuously. "I thought that would be about your breed."

Lockjaw spoke for the first time. "If he won't shoot, why not beat him up, Lance? Me? I wouldn't ask nothin' better than to skin him up so he'd look like the star-spangled banner."

"Please!" Alma's tone was firm now, even indignant. "I think there's been enough of this. Haven't any of you any regard for a woman?"

Blake sneered. "Too much, maybe," he amended. "But the lady's right—there's enough palaver. I'm goin' to take pleasure in meeting you one by one if you're lucky enough to stay out of jail, and finding out whether you're as brave as you talk when you're in a bunch. Meanwhile, get off my land. Come in, Alma." He turned and walked into the house, without looking back.

Alma stood hesitant a moment, evidently thinking fast. When her husband had gotten out of earshot, she said rapidly to Flint: "He's got to be in town at midnight. Could your friend, Doc, come then?"

"Ma'am," Flint told her earnestly, "we'll come any time you say. It don't make no difference whether your husband is there or not."

She held out her hand to him swiftly. "Thank you," she said. "Come at midnight!" Then with a nod to the others and a word to Pearson she followed her husband toward the house.

The four men stood looking after her a moment. Then Pearson said: "I reckon it ain't in order for me to be thankin' you two, but I'd like you to know that I think you're plenty white, all of you—white, clear through to the inside of the gizzard!"

They rode together toward town.

"How come a lady like her ever got married to a human centipede like that?" Lockjaw asked, voicing the question which had been in Flint's mind also.

"I guess he just come at the right time," Pearson answered slowly. "She'd just lost her husband—the father of the little girl. She was a woman, alone, with nobody to look after the spread. This Blake showed up about then, brought in by Bogart, and I guess he can be right persuasive when it's to his interest to be. I reckon that's the only explanation—and at that it's still a mystery."

"Like most things connected with women," Lance commented sagely.

"What I can't make out," Pearson said reflectively, "is how he come to let the spread run down so. I can't believe he hasn't got savvy enough to run it right. It was clear when he got it, and in three years he's managed to slap a mortgage onto it and get himself in such a hole he's liable to lose it."

"Who'll get it if he does?" Flint asked. "The bank," Pearson said curtly. "And that's Bogart."

Flint looked grim. "This whole set-up begins to smell stronger and stronger to me all the time," he growled.

A rider came toward them at a good pace, set spurs to his mount, and passed them at a gallop. Lance exchanged a glance with Flint. Pearson started to speak but Lance shook his head, frowning. Lockjaw hadn't recognized the rider and Lance didn't want him to know. The man was one of those who had been playing seven-up at the nearby table when Lockjaw made his break.

CHAPTER 7
THE SECRET VAULT

PEARSON LEFT them before they reached town, turning off toward his ranch. "I'll see you out there at midnight," he said. "Good luck!"

"No call for you to do that, Pearson," Flint told him. "There's no tellin' what kind of a jackpot we'll be in out there. No sense in your gettin' mixed up in it. You have to live around here—we don't."

"I reckon I've already been declared in on it. Wouldn't be any use my tryin' to back out now—and I don't want to."

"A man's known by the company he keeps, fella. You can't afford to put yourself outside the law. Anyway, there's enough of us. One more gun wouldn't do us any good whatever."

"One more gun is one more gun," said Pearson stubbornly. "I won't go in with you on the other thing, but I'll be out there at midnight." And he rode off.

In town they collected Doc and Charlie and told them what had happened at the ranch.

Doc frowned. "Sounds bad for the youngster," he commented. "Pallor, difficulty in breathing, abdominal distension. It may be necessary to operate right away. Flint, you'd better circulate around and find me some chloroform. One of the stores handles drugs, I think—the one just the other side of the hotel."

Charlie Parr had been looking thoughtful. "Doc," he said now, "if that little girl dies after you've operated on her, you're goin' to be in a jackpot—the worst jackpot even you have ever been in."

Doc Grimson looked at him with one eye-brow raised. "I'd hang for it if they got me. What would you do in my place?" His voice was level, unemotional.

Charlie looked embarrassed. "That ain't a fair question," he answered irritably.

"You're the one to take the chance. Blamed if I see any reason why you should do it."

"You and the rest of the boys are going to be in it, too," Doc pointed out. "Maybe you don't realize what you're getting into. I haven't got any right to practice—here. And if I did have, the little girl's legal father has forbidden me to see her. If she dies under the knife or afterwards, it'll be pretty close to murder. And you'll be helping. Only the law will never hang us. Everybody in this county, and everybody in this state white, black or yellow, will be on our trail. They'll skin us alive and nail our bare skins up beside our carcasses. You ought to know that as well as I do."

Charlie looked like a man who was very sorry he had said anything. "Shucks, Doc," he said uncomfortably, "I reckon I spoke out of turn. You know we're behind you every minute, don't you? I wasn't aimin' for to save my own hide. It's about wore out, anyhow."

Doc smiled slightly. "What about you, Lance?"

Lance stared at him. "Fellas has been laid up for months," he said, "for askin' me questions like that."

"How about you, Lockjaw?"

"Hunh?"

"We're likely to get a lynching for going out there. There's no reason why you should take the risk."

Lockjaw burst into a sudden bray of laughter. "Lynchin', huh? Shucks, they been tryin' to hang me an' Charlie so long we done got rope-burn just from thinkin' about it."

Doc chuckled. "All right then," he said. "Charlie and I have been looking over the bank. We better get at that first. It won't take long. Lockjaw, you'll go and get the nags. Wait about five minutes after we start, then bring them along quietly around in the back of that shed behind the bank. Hold them there until we come out. The rest of us will go in. Lance, you'll keep watch out of the front windows and Flint at the rear door. Here Flint comes now.... Did you get that chloroform?... good! Now we'll split up and wander around casually to that shed where Lockjaw is going to bring the nags. Get there as soon as you can, but don't attract any attention."

Lance got Doc aside and told him about meeting the card-player from the saloon. Doc nodded. "Charlie and I guessed it." he said. "But Blake won't be expecting anything so early. We'll likely get through before he wakes up to it."

A few moments later they assembled again under the shadowy obscurity of the shed.

"There's a watchman," Doc whispered. "His regular beat is

around the bank on the outside. We want to get him without making any noise and without hurting him more than necessary. Lance, that right fist of yours is like a pile-driver. Suppose you take the watchman on. Better play drunk, hadn't you?"

LANCE NODDED. His pulses were already beginning to pound with excitement. Trouble which walked by day he could meet with equanimity, but this night work always got to him. The furtiveness, the stealth, his own soft, secret movement, woke something savage in him—some age-old thrill of the predatory man.

He walked off softly to the right behind a darkened building, from the corner of which he could watch the alley behind the bank. He would watch until the watchman came on that part of his beat, then…. But the man was already there, seated on the steps leading to the rear door of the bank, smoking a cigarette.

He drew a deep breath. This part of the town was silent, deserted. The stealthiness which had begun, already, to gather in him, made it seem impossible, somehow, to break the silence. His instinct was to sneak up on the man—and that would have been fatal.

He staggered out into the alleyway and broke into song, letting his voice drawl off-key, drunkenly:

"Oh, bury me not on the lone prairie…."

It sounded false, forced, unnatural to his ears. The watchman would never be taken in by it.

But the man had not moved, except to turn his head idly in

Lance's direction. Lance rolled on toward him, breaking his song from time to time to hiccup loudly.

"Those hiccups sound like somebody drawing nails," he thought. "I'm goin' to have trouble with him. If I bungle this…."

"Fling a handful of roses o'er my grave."

He pulled up, teetering, before the watchman. "Hey, pardner, gimme l'il piece fire, will ya?" he requested. "I ain't had smoke—hic—f'r more'n an hour.

"Los' all m' matches down at the faro layout, bettin' 'em against Croakey Joe's di'mon's." He assumed a tone of dignified solemnity. "Pardner, take advice 'v an older feller—hic—don' never buck no faro layout."

The watchman chuckled. "I'm kind of shy of matches myself," he said rising, "You better take a light from this."

Lance's right fist moved nine inches, like a striking snake.

"Sorry, pardner," he muttered.

The crack of his knuckles against the point of the watchman's jaw sounded loud in his ears.

The man's head snapped back; his knees buckled; he started to slump to the ground. Lance caught him and eased him down.

"Dirty trick, old timer," he said softly to the unconscious form. "I'll have to send you a quart of red-eye for that, some time."

The others came over from the shed, Doc Grimson knelt and took the keys from the watchman, selected one swiftly, and a second later the back door swung open. He motioned for them to come and carry the unconscious form inside.

Lance and Flint bound and gagged him, while Doc and Charlie slipped forward to the vaults. A few seconds later Lance followed them, leaving Flint at the rear door.

He went to the front windows and crouched, scanning the street.

Immediately in front there was little movement. The saloons and gambling houses were farther down the street; the stores across the way were closed and dark. A miner reeled down the street, as drunk, evidently as Lance had previously appeared to be, and disappeared into the darkness. A group of punchers from a nearby spread pounded by on their way out of town. From behind him, Lance could hear no sound. He might just as well have been alone in the bank for all the noise Doc and Charlie were making.

A glance over his shoulder showed him only the faintest glimmer of light, scarcely discernible even from where he crouched. But it told him certainly that the others were at work, there in the obscurity behind the counter. Two riders appeared suddenly out of the darkness, coming into town. They came at a gallop, the hoof-beats muffled in the soft dust of the street, but just before they came to the bank they slowed down.

Lance, his pulses suddenly jumping, watched them go by. They were the card-player from the saloon and Blake! He had no doubt of it whatever, even though the light was dim. Passing, they both looked hard at the bank. When they had gotten by, they increased speed again.

So Lockjaw's outbreak back there in the saloon really had roused suspicion! Lance's immediate impulse was to let the others know. He made his way softly back to where the light showed dimly, but the scene which met his eyes checked the speech on his lips, held him silent.

DOC GRIMSON knelt before the door of a small vault— really no more than a good-sized safe built into the wall. The thumb and first fingers of his right hand were on the knob of the combination, his ear close to the lock. His face, in the glow of a dark-lantern which was three quarters shuttered, showed as a shadowy mask of concentration. The eyes glinted, withdrawn, sightless; the lips hung slightly parted; the shoulders, chest, throat, all were motionless as though the man had ceased to breathe. And Lance knew that Doc Grimson for the moment had become only two sensitive, infinitely delicate fingers and an inner ear, cut off from all sound, all consciousness of movement, other than the shadowy, inaudible click of the tumblers as they fell into place.

Softly, Lance withdrew again to the window. The street in front was deserted. He tried to think what Blake would do. Perhaps he would make the rounds of the saloons first, looking for them, with the idea of keeping them in sight and trapping them if they undertook to rob the bank. Failing to find them, what would be his next course? Would he come directly to the bank? Lance doubted it. Blake was cold-blooded, shrewd. He would not risk going up against all five of them unless he had plenty of help at his shoulder. He would stop first to gather his men, and then make his investigation. If he was smart, he'd plan to spot his men around, under cover, and wait for developments. But as soon as he got to the bank, the absence of the watchman would make him suspect that it had already been entered. Lockjaw ought to be warned.

A soft exclamation from behind him drew his attention. He slipped back in time to see the door of the vault swinging open.

The excitement of that drove everything else from his mind for a second. He watched while Doc took the lamp from Charlie and, stooping a little, entered the vault. The lantern-glow revealed several ordinary filing cabinets the drawers of which proved to be locked. While Doc set deftly about opening them, Lance told what he had seen.

"Better hurry, Doc," Charlie Parr said calmly. "Lance, you go on back and let us know if anybody shows up."

Doc Grimson had scarcely appeared to listen. He was absorbed in the examination of the drawers.

Lance went back to his window. Outside, nothing had changed. Down the street an oil lamp, attached to the side of the building cast a dim glow, cut alternations of light and shadow on the dust of roadway. From farther down there came, faintly audible, the sounds of laughter and a tin-pan beat of music.

They were going to make it, he thought jubilantly. Blake had been nothing but a false alarm.

Then a slight movement in the shadows between the two buildings across the way caught his eye. Looking closely, he could make out the figure of a man, crouching. Behind him was another, standing close alongside the building, his figure almost merging with the shadowy wall.

Lance's gaze darted to the other corners of the buildings. Nothing there, apparently. But yes! A stir of movement at the far end, a man slouched openly into view, leaned against the corner of the building. That made four that he could see. Blake was playing it wisely. They were surrounded!

He slipped back to the others. "Four men hiding between the houses across the street," he whispered tensely. "Blake's got us hemmed in."

Charlie Parr stiffened, turning instinctively toward the dim rectangles made by the front windows. Doc Grimson folded the paper in his hands and began to gather up others which he stuffed in his pockets. What was left over after his pockets were filled, he handed to Lance and Charlie.

Flint appeared out of the darkness.

"Crowd of men in the back," he whispered, "closing in from both sides."

Doc Grimson turned out the light. Charlie Parr said: "This Blake used his head, didn't he?" His voice held a note of bitterness.

"He was faster than I thought he'd be," Doc admitted grimly.

"We've got to get out some other way," Flint said. "There are enough of them outside there to blow us to hell if we step out of the doorway."

"They're in front, too." Lance told him. "That means they must have formed a circle around us."

"Two things to do." Doc breathed curtly. "Pick the weakest side and come out shooting, or give up. The first idea means that we'll likely kill somebody. Whatever we do, we'll have to hurry. Somebody is sure to stumble on Lockjaw and the horses pretty soon."

CHAPTER 8
LOCKJAW TREES A TOWN

THE OTHERS were silent a long moment. This was one of the problems their way of life was continually putting up to them. The men outside were evidently a posse of citizens gathered by Blake. Killing one of them would not only make the charge against them murder, it would put on their conscience the one thing most repugnant to them—the death of a decent man whose only offense was upholding the law. The alternative was long years in prison, with the chance, always, of dancing from the end of a rope. For the very men they sought to spare might make them the victims of mob blood-lust.

"They're askin' for it," Flint said, his voice hard.

Lance knew suddenly that he was thinking of a youngster, across whose tender small body an iron-shod wheel had brutally passed. Nothing else could have put that note of ruthlessness in his voice. For Flint, of them all, had perhaps the strongest instinctive feeling for law and order.

He knew in the second of silence which followed that the other four must be staring toward the speaker in surprise. Perhaps they were reading the secret thought behind Flint's words, and felt, like Lance, a little shock of astonishment at the idea that it was still their duty to get help to that little girl. But it seemed impossible now.

If they got out of this alive, the whole town would be on their heels, and they would have exactly the same freedom of action as driven rabbits. Somehow, unthinkably, it remained necessary for them to twist and turn until they could go to the help of a woman and a child who could look for help to no one else. It was mad, impossible, absurd—and it had to be done!

And while the realization of that raced through Lance's brain, he became aware suddenly that the air about him was in movement. An instant before it had been still, now it moved, slipping past the skin of his face, touching his hands like the soft curl of dark water. The back door had been opened.

He felt Doc Grimson's quick hand on his arm, sensed the tense immobility of the others. There was something—an almost inaudible rustle which told him that someone was moving along the corridor that led from the back door, through the inner office, into the main room where they stood. That must be Blake. Blake had more nerve than anybody had given him credit for. He could have waited outside and cut down on them as they came out. It wasn't necessary to risk coming in after them.

Lance thought that almost absently. Actually he was absorbed by an entirely trivial problem. Where had the draft come from? Just opening a door didn't make a draft like that. Funny, it looked like a pretty tight, well-made building.

An actual noise in the hallway back of the office sounded loud in his ears. It was the only indication he had that his nerves that taut and strained, that so slight a noise could strike his ear-drums so sharply. And then he was aware that someone—not the man who had made the sound—was standing in the doorway not ten feet from them. Standing motionless.

It was going to be hell, fighting in that darkness. They wouldn't be able to keep together. It would be every man for himself and the devil take the hindmost.

A little gust of air blew directly into his face, and he turned his head. At the far end of the room, in the ceiling he saw a single star twinkle faintly, then the meaning of the star dawned on him. There was a skylight—a little one—at that end of the room, and it was open.

Lance's spine prickled. Somebody was up there and even as he looked the star disappeared and there was the faintest scraping, as though a body was slipping through.

LANCE TOOK Doc's chin in his palm and turned Doc's head silently toward the skylight. Doc nodded his head, then Doc's lips were at his ear. "We'll go out that way." It was not a whisper. It was speech that materialized somehow inside Lance's ear, almost without having been spoken. The lips disappeared from his ear and he knew Doc had moved to tell the others. The star in the skylight reappeared, disappeared again. Whoever was coming in was clumsy. Unseen feet tapped hard on the counter.

A voice from a corner in front of Lance said: "We know you're there—better give up—you haven't a chance." It must have been the man in the doorway, who had moved to that corner.

No one answered. At Doc's touch, Lance began to move toward the skylight and the men who had entered by it. They must get those two men and then get to the roof. Lance knew that he would have to be first to go through the opening. The marshal's men must have left somebody on the roof—somebody who would be waiting with a gun to shoot the first man to come up. The others would have to use both hands to get up. He, Lance, could chin himself with his left and use his right to shoot with.

The man in the corner said in a hoarse undertone: "Light a lantern, Jed, and stick it around the doorway there. Keep out of sight."

There was what appeared to be a moment of hesitation during which the man Jed was remembering, possibly, that the partition which made the inner office was thin. Then the doorway came into dim relief as a match flared. Lance saw no more.

He gave all his attention to trying to locate the men who had come in through the skylight. The light from the inner room did nothing to help him, but he knew that once the lantern was put around the door, he himself would be silhouetted against it—an easy target for guns in front of him. He had to get them before the light showed him up.

For the moment it was the others who were at a disadvantage. A dim glimmer of starlight came down through the open trap. It showed him a hint of the head and shoulders of one of the men. A scraping noise to the right of that one told him that the clumsy one was crouching below the counter.

Then things happened fast. Jed must have started putting the lantern around the door, for there was a momentary glimmer of light on the man before him, and Lance saw his gun flash up. Lance struck for the man's wrist just as a Colt behind him smashed the silence in a deafening roar and Jed's lantern went out in a tinkle of shattered glass.

It went out too fast. Lance's blow, started in the light and finished in the darkness, missed the other's wrist. The ring of steel on steel told him that he had struck down the barrel of the man's gun and the jumping roar of the Colt told him he had failed to knock it out of his hand. He closed in striking for the head; missed, felt his six gun hit shoulder flesh. He groped for the man's gun hand, caught instead the numbing crack of steel across his right temple.

Behind him the room was a bedlam of staccato thunder as guns laced the darkness with flame. The acrid smoke of powder was suffocating in his nostrils. His left hand caught the barrel at his temple as a man might catch a stinging wasp, held it as his knees sagged. With his right he struck blindly, heard his gun-barrel smack against bone, felt the man before him give and slowly crumple to the floor.

He staggered, trying to shake his head clear. Beside him, was the grunting scuffling of two locked in a death struggle on the floor. He dove at the sound, felt flesh, groped, found the upper man mustached. "Charlie?" he asked.

"No; Doc!" the response was gasped from the man underneath.

Lance slipped a half hammer-lock under the mustached man's chin, and snapped him back downwards on the floor. The man grunted, tried to drive his knee into Lance's belly. Lance caught him by the throat, lifted his head, and smashed it to the floor. The man went limp. To lengthen his sleep, Lance drew his gun and clipped him neatly with it.

The room had grown suddenly silent. From the corner where the first man had spoken came the clicking sound of cartridge sliding into the chambers of a Colt. It came to Lance suddenly that all this endless fight in the dark had taken place in the time it had taken to empty a couple of six-guns!

There was a yell from outside. A gun barked. Somebody shouted: "The horses! We got their horses!"

"There's a feller with 'em," somebody else yelled: "Get him!"

A sharp fusillade followed and ended when a voice shouted, "He's down. Quit shootin' or you'll stampede 'em!"

Lance jumped to the counter. They had to get these horses. He reached upward, got a grip of the trap door with his left hand and pulled up, Colt ready in his right hand. As he did so, there was a thunder of hoofs behind the bank and he almost groaned aloud.

The horses were gone!

Orange flame spurted from the far corner as a gun blasted the silence. Lead bit at Lance's side like a striking snake. He heaved himself, Colt first, through the opening, conscious as he did so that another gun had spoken, followed by a clatter and a curse from close to him.

A MAN was on the roof, but apparently that man was not watching the skylight. He had run over to look at the excitement at the rear. Lance strode toward him softly. The man turned, froze, as Lance whispered: "One move an' you're dead!"

Lance took the gun, then apologizing for the second time that night, connected his right fist with his captive's jaw.

When he turned again, Charlie Parr was coming up from the opening. Below him somebody was fanning a gun at irregular intervals.

"That's Doc," Charlie explained, dryly. "He shot Blake's gun out of his hand and now he's keeping him too busy to get it. I guess Blake only took time to load one of 'em."

Flint heaved up through the opening and bent down to say in a low voice, "All right, Doc."

"Where are all the others?" Lance asked puzzled. "It sounded like they had an army in there."

"The others took a likin' for the inner room," Charlie told him. "We had to damage a couple of 'em and the rest of 'em got kind of discouraged. That Blake, though, was hard to hit."

Doc Grimson came up through the opening as, from below, Blake's voice rang out furiously. "They're on the roof. Get after 'em."

"Keep down," Doc directed, "while I pick the side to get out on."

He had scarcely spoken before there was a sudden thud and rush of hoofs from up the alleyway behind the bank. A bunch of five horses came careening down that narrow way at full gallop. On the leading horse was a figure gone wild. He was standing erect in his stirrups and fanning his mount with his sombrero like a man making a fancy ride.

"Whoopee!" he yelled as the five horses smashed past the bank, "Here they are, boys! Where do you want 'em?"

"Why dang me," Charlie Parr remarked mildly. "If it ain't old Lockjaw!"

"Around in front, Lockjaw," Doc yelled. "Bring 'em around in front!"

His yell brought a scattering volley from the men in the rear who had stampeded out of the way of the racing horses, but the angle was bad and the shots did no harm.

Lockjaw and his led-bunch swerved around the building next door at break-neck speed and an instant later emerged into the street. "Whoopee!" yelled Lockjaw ecstatically. "Hump yo'selves, broncos. Yip, yip, yi-yi-yi!"

By this time the main street was a milling mob of excited citizens, attracted by the firing and rushing toward the bank to see what had happened. Not many of them had reached the danger zone yet but they were on their way. There were really only the four men who had been stationed between the building across the street to stop that wild charge of Lockjaw's. Unwisely, they stepped out from their shadows to do so.

"Try not to kill anybody," Doc warned, and shot the hat from the foremost man's head.

Lance slung a shot at the second man's gun-arm; the bullet went high and smashed his shoulder. He swore, then took his time with the next shot—so much time that there wasn't any next shot. Doc and Flint had both fired, just as Lockjaw pulled up in a cloud of dust.

Lance heard Doc Grimson laugh happily and saw him leap from the roof and land in his saddle without touching the ground. Lance's own horse, a magnificent bay stallion he had collected from one Ed Lowery, crooked rancher, was too far from the roof for such acrobatics. Lance hit the dirt, flung a warning shot at a couple of men from the rear who were foolish enough to poke their heads around the bank building, and hit the saddle running.

The crowd in the street, he saw, had disappeared with great suddenness. A second later the stallion had leapt into a dead run, racing the other four down the dusty street into the darkness of the countryside. Lance rode bent low in the saddle to escape the wild volley that hummed over their heads as the besiegers in the rear of the bank got into action. So did the others, with the exception of Lockjaw.

That horse-faced hombre, who had apparently been eating loco weed, brought up the rear, riding erect, waving his sombrero, and yelling insults over his shoulder at the town of Tarpaulin.

"You can't shoot, you wall-eyed centipedes," bellowed Lockjaw, "You can't shoot for beans!"

CHAPTER 9
AT BLAKE'S RANCH

ALMA BLAKE lived through the minutes before midnight in a state of almost intolerable tension. The various emotions of the day had been enough to completely exhaust her and she was living now really "on her nerves"—nerves frayed by successive strain and tension which had swept mercilessly across a mind already tortured by a constantly increasing fear for Julie.

Her growing revolt against Blake's cold brutality had crystallized into hatred after the scene with Flint Maddox and the others. When she followed him to the house it was to go at once to her little girl's bedside, to busy herself frantically with cold applications and other medicaments to relieve the child's suffering.

Blake had begun on her then in his cold, venomous voice, insulting her, sneering at her, lashing her as though his tongue were a knotted thong. She stood it in silence for a while, only half-conscious, indeed, of the things he was saying to her. Then, as much to her own surprise as his, she flared out at him, easing her furious heart of the burden of contempt, and anger and hatred which had been building up in her through long months.

And then Blake had struck her, with the flat of his hand, violently. The blow knocked her off her feet, left her dazed and strangely numbed, feeling neither pain nor resentment.

"Get up, you slut," he had raged at her, jerking her upright, "I'll show you how to talk to me!"

A rider had come up then, saving her from further violence, and Blake, going out, had held a low-toned conference with him. A moment later they had ridden off together. Blake had appeared excited, with a cruel, half-triumphant flare in his eyes which convinced her that he had found a way to vent his spite on someone. After a little, she wondered if it might be the five strangers, and she prayed that it wasn't. But for the time being she was incapable even of that thought.

Not even Blake had ever raised his hand to her before. She knew that she ought to be unbearably humiliated and furious, but she still felt nothing, except a sort of wonder that anything like that could actually have happened to her. And that being so, her first thought was curious. She thought: "I should have killed him before he went out. Then, at least, he couldn't have killed any of the others."

It was as though, thinking that, she thought also that Blake had already killed her and her child.

Julie's groaning brought her back to a sense of the situation and the child's needs. She realized then that, if only they knew of it, the outlaw-doctor could have come then—he need not wait until midnight. But she had no way to send him word.

She became obsessed by the possibility that he might see her husband in town and so come earlier, just a little earlier. She kept going to the door to see. But the night greeted her with nothing but darkness and silence.

Julie had relapsed into a state of semiconsciousness which, though if might be merciful in relieving her pain, drove fear still deeper into her mother's heart. The child was deathly pale, breathing with difficulty. Her eyes half-open, showing the whites. The childish chubbiness of her face seemed to have disappeared, leaving the features drawn but aetherially delicate, as though the spirit were already showing itself, preparatory to taking flight.

An owl hooted low and mournfully from a tree along the ravine. Far off, the eery, long-drawn howl of a wolf lifted itself toward the watching stars. The old-fashioned clock on the mantel struck the half-hour; its soft, single, solemn note like a warning. And Alma knew suddenly that Julie would die.

She put her head into her hands and began to cry in low choked sobs. "My baby—Oh, my baby girl!" she said over and over. "Oh, my baby darling—my little one—Julie! Julie!"

But after a while revolt strengthened her, and she sat, dry-eyed, feverish, telling herself that this thing was impossible, that help must come, that this unendurable anguish must turn out to be no more than a nightmare, to disappear with the dawn and the clean, sane light of day.

Only, the fear in her heart kept telling her that it was not so. These men, these strangers who had been the cause of injuring her child, would not come. So the minutes dragged on.... Then a sudden beat of hoofs on the road turned off toward the house, and Alma got up suddenly, knees weak, hands at her pulsing throat.

There was only one rider. What had happened? Was it her husband coming back?

SHE STOOD paralyzed, incapable of movement or speech, while the rider dismounted and strode toward the door. His knock roused her to the possibility of speech only. "Come in!" she cried, her voice suddenly urgent, trembling. It could not be her husband, otherwise he would not have knocked.

The door swung open and Jud Pearson stood there, silent. But his expression told her that the news he had was bad.

She found herself saying: "It's bad! They're not coming. Jud! Oh, Jud!"

He came toward her, his eyes full of pity and put his arms around her. But she held him off, with her hands against his chest.

"Tell me," she commanded, her voice suddenly quiet. "What has happened?"

"I'm afraid it's pretty bad, Alma," he said gently. "They—

they've got half the town on their trail tonight. There ain't a chance that they can make it here."

"What happened, Jud?"

"They tried to rob the bank."

Alma stood stunned, unbelieving. "They tried to rob the bank!" The words rang in her ears with an air of unreality. They didn't make sense. Her mind couldn't take them in. "They tried to rob the bank!"

Suddenly, she began to laugh. She couldn't stop herself. The childishness, the triviality of it, was too much to stand. A life had waited on them—a life like Julie's! And they had stopped to rob a bank! Men were children—careless, cruel, trivial-minded children. You trusted them, you depended on them, looked up to them, and they did this sort of thing to you. The irresponsibility of it! The callous, stupid cruelty of it. She sat down in her chair and laughed, hysterically.

Vaguely, she was conscious of Jud's voice, alarmed, full of consternation. "Don't, Alma—don't, darling. You—you mustn't."

He thought her mind had given way under the strain. But it hadn't. Her mind never had been clearer, never had seen life and men so wholly and so plainly. She thought she had better try to explain to Jud. It really was too funny!

"I m-made her," she got out between spasms of laughter. "M-months under my heart. With my blood. B-but it amuses them to rob a bank! D-don't you see it, Jud—don't you see?"

It was really very funny. She would like him to see just how funny it was. And suddenly she got up. She wasn't laughing any more. Her eyes were blazing with a light not altogether sane.

"Like cruel, stupid boys—smutting life over with their silly guns and their fighting and their greediness and stupid, stupid games. I waited for them—do you hear that? I waited for them.—Why didn't they come?"

Jud Pearson looked concerned, abashed. "You—you mustn't take it so hard, Alma," he said uncomfortably. "Maybe—maybe it'll come out all right, anyway."

"Why didn't they come?"

"It wasn't really so bad, Alma, I guess. Looks like they was lookin' for something against Bogart. They didn't go into anything but his vault. Maybe they thought that if they couldn't come out here until midnight, they might as well put in the time tryin' to protect themselves. Your hus—er—Blake trapped 'em."

"Why did you come?" Alma taunted him, "Why didn't you rob a bank, too? Or find some flies and pull its wings off?"

She saw with bitter satisfaction how much she had hurt him. Well, he was a man, wasn't he? What did it matter? Julie was going to die. She began to cry then. The great sobs came up in her throat, tearing at her bosom.

Jud Pearson came to her and put his arms around her. With a sudden rush of remorse, she let her head fall on his shoulder. "I—I'm sorry, Jud," she sobbed. "Please—forgive me. Julie…."

Jud interrupted her gently. "Don't, Alma. It don't matter. I—love you, Alma. I've always loved you. I'll always want to stand by you."

She let herself go then, crying against his chest and saying over and over again: "It hurts—it hurts so! I needed them—I needed them!"

She heard no sound to warn her. She was aware of a presence in the doorway only when Jud stiffened and, turning, took his arms from her. Then she looked up and, there, picked out by the light of the single lamp which lighted the room dimly, stood a man—a slender man of middle height and middle age, soberly dressed, an extraordinarily graceful-looking man, who wore two guns strapped low on his thighs, and who stood and looked at her with a pair of gray eyes which were luminous with intelligence and understanding.

"Oh!" The cry was torn from her throat in a sudden great wave of exaltation. "You've come!"

And as she spoke she became aware that the old-fashioned clock on the mantel was striking, the mellow notes ringing solemnly, tenderly, against the silence which followed her cry. It was midnight.

CHAPTER 10
LIFE FOR LIFE

THEY FILED in, all five of them, dusty, like men who had ridden hard. To Alma, looking at them with that sudden exaltation in her heart, they looked more than life-size. They came in so quietly and so sure of themselves. It was impossible to believe, just seeing them, that what Jud had said was true. Bank-robbers, chased by half a town, could not act like this.

But Doc Grimson's first words dispelled any doubts she might have had about the risk they were taking. "If you don't mind, ma'am," she said. "We'll close up a little." He made a gesture to the others and they moved quietly to the windows and began to close the shutters. Doc himself went directly to Julie's cot, which Alma had put in the living room.

Alma was about to follow when she felt Flint's eyes upon her and realized that she had not thanked him, nor the others, for coming.

Jud Pearson spoke before the words on her lips took form. "You mean they're still on your trail?" he asked. "You haven't thrown them off?"

It was Lance Clayton who answered. "You can't ever tell," he said in his slow musical voice. "We run into a couple of pilgrims just after we left the trail and began to circle back in this direction. If they talk, it may save the posse some time."

"We'd ought to have seen that they didn't talk," Lockjaw grumbled gloomily. "If Doc had've *let* me—" He stopped embarrassed suddenly by Alma's presence.

She realized vaguely that he meant the two men should have been killed, but her mind was too taken up by the look on Flint's face to really take the thought in. Flint had looked at her with simple friendliness and warmth when he had come in, but now that he had turned away she caught a momentary expression of sadness and suffering in his features which surprised and troubled her. Her woman's intuition told her that the look had something to do with her, and then she remembered that she

Suddenly the room was filled with the thunder
of six-guns and rifles as Doc Grimson bent
over the small, unconscious form of Julie.

had been in Jud Pearson's arms when the five had arrived. Flint
must have seen her when Doc Grimson opened the door.

The thought that she might cause him suffering struck at
her heart. And for a moment she wondered if she were so sure,
wondered whether, if this man showed he wanted her…. But
she shot the thought aside, with a sense of disloyalty to Jud.
She knew that in those moments before the others came, she
had surrendered her heart to Jud unreservedly. The fact that she

had not avowed it in words made no difference. She had meant it, and she knew that the man who held her in his arms had sensed it.

Following on this swift passage of thought, she remembered, with a little sense of horror, that after all she was a married woman. But the sentiment, she felt at once, was superficial. Blake had somehow ceased to exist for her, except as a menace. There was no longer any reality in their relationship.

"Pearson, you've got no business being here." It was Flint

who had turned and addressed the man at her side. "If Blake turns up at the head of that posse, you'll be in a bad jam."

Jud looked grim. "I reckon I'll just have to risk that," he drawled. "It won't be any worse for me than for you fellers."

"Yes, it will," Flint said. "You've made your life here—got your spread here. Being in this deal will put you outside the law. You'll lose everything."

"That's right," Lance Clayton put in quickly. "We're already in bad in lots of places. That's our life. It just ain't good sense for you to throw everything you've got away on a little deal like this. Show some sense fella, and high-tail it before it's too late. You can't do any good here."

"Sure!" Jud said indignantly. "My spread is worth more than your lives, huh? Thanks. I'm stickin'!"

Flint went to him and put a hard hand on his shoulder. "Listen, Jud," he said earnestly. "You're a square hombre, but you're not thinkin', fella. You've got somebody else to consider besides yourself. If you get outlawed, who's goin' to—look after Alm—Mrs. Blake. Don't think I'm tryin' to horn into your affairs, but this is no time to beat around the bush. You keep clear of this; keep yourself clear to help her. I'm thinkin' that before another day is over, she's not goin' to have anybody else—I mean, she might be needin' you," he finished hastily. But Alma knew, as did the others, that he meant that Blake would not live long.

PEARSON, SHE could see, was plainly shaken by this argument, but, after a moment's thought, he shook his head.

"It just ain't in the cards," he said stubbornly. "Alma needs help now, as much as she ever will. I'm stickin'."

Flint sighed and looked at Lance. "I'll take care of it, Flint," the latter said gently. "You go on out and keep a watch down the road."

Flint shrugged, said "Thanks, Lance," and went out, his shoulders sagging a little as though he were suddenly very weary. Lance followed him with his eyes, and Alma realized that Lance, too, believed that Flint cared for her—enough to sacrifice his own desires for her happiness. But, curiously, it was not Flint's regard for her which caught at her heart. It was the relationship between the two men which moved her. "Why—why, they love one another!" she thought, astonished.

It seemed a funny word to use about men—especially about men as tough as these men were. But it was the word to use, all right. No woman could have looked with more tenderness and understanding than this lean-hipped, big-shouldered young man had looked after his friend.

Her glance went back to Lance. He was looking thoughtfully at the back of his right hand, examining, apparently, the skin over his knuckles which looked split. He must have knocked his hand against something.

He frowned a little, sighed slightly, then walked over to Jud and put his left hand on his shoulder.

"Jud," he said, "You'll do to take along. I'm sorry, pardner, that we can't take you this time."

His right hand lifted, like the head of a striking snake. The clenched knuckles landed with the impact of a catapulted rock, just a little to the left of the point of Jud Pearson's jaw. Jud's head snapped back, his knees buckled; Lance caught him, eased him gently to the floor.

"Oh!" Alma breathed wide-eyed, her hands at her throat.

"Sorry, ma'am," Lance apologized, "but it was the only way, an' he ain't hurt much."

Alma said "Oh," again, faintly, but in a different tone.

"There's two things we can do," Lance said, "keep him here or tie him on his bronc and send him toward his spread. If you've got a place to hide him where your husband ain't likely to look, it'd be better to pack Jud in there. Then, when things settle down and the coast is clear, you can untie and set him loose."

"He—he'd be safe in the clothes closet in my room, I think."

"Fine. Help me tie him up, Lockjaw."

Alma found Doc Grimson at her elbow. He looked grave. "I'm sorry to tell you, Mrs. Blake," he said, "but your little girl's case won't wait until morning. She has got to be operated on now."

Anguish clutched again at Alma's heart, and a sense of horror that in the drama of the situation around her, she had for a moment forgotten Julie.

"Do you mean—is it bad? Can you save her, Doctor?"

"I think so. But I can't promise anything. She should have had attention hours ago. Everything now depends on how much blood she has lost. There's an internal hemorrhage—hepatic almost certainly. It is an extremely, slow one—otherwise she would not be alive now. I think it is not too late. Do you want me to go ahead?"

"Oh, please—yes!"

The assent came unhesitatingly, out of a confidence so complete that Alma did not even realize that it was strange.

"I'll need hot water, then—lots of it."

"It's already ready. I—I put in on the stove hours ago, thinking you might...."

"Good. Let's get busy. I'm going to need you to help me. It's not going to be pleasant. Will you be brave enough for it?"

Alma said "yes" to that, but she watched him with a heart beating so hard it nearly choked her as he opened a black case and began to lay out instruments, cotton and bandages.

Under his directions she found a low table and covered it with a sheet. Onto this table he lifted Julie. Then he opened a bottle, and Alma caught the unmistakable odor of chloroform.

The door behind her opened, closed. She heard Flint's voice say quietly: "The posse's here. They've stopped out on the road with a lantern. I reckon they can't miss our sign."

ALMA CAUGHT her breath. She turned to Doc Grimson, panic-stricken, pleading. "Oh, don't go—please! Let me talk to them. I can tell them—persuade them. They won't let my little girl die! They'll give you another chance to get away! Please—*please* let me try!"

Doc Grimson said simply: "Don't worry, Mrs. Blake. You can talk to them, but we're going to stay anyway. Julie will have her chance."

Charlie Parr appeared suddenly in the kitchen doorway, and

Alma realized for the first time that he had left the house by the rear door as soon as he had entered.

"They're movin' to surround the house," said Charlie. "This Blake plays 'em close to his belt, all right. And he's smart."

Lance's voice came suddenly from one of the bedroom windows. "That's far enough, Blake," he called out sharply. "Better get back under cover."

There was the muffled sound of a curse from outside, half of surprise, and half that of a man who has verified a guess. Then Blake's voice came: "You fellers had better give up. We've got you surrounded."

Lance laughed. "You had us that way once before, hombre," he drawled. "It don't seem to do you much good."

"All right, Mrs. Blake," Doc Grimson said with a hint of irony, "this is where you make your talk."

Alma went to the door and flung it wide. "These men have come here to help my little girl," she said, lifting her voice clearly. "She's got to be operated on to save her life, and they have risked their lives to let Doc Grimson do it. If you're men, you won't interfere. If you're men, you'll wait and give them at least a chance to get away. Won't you do that—won't you think of your own children and do that for me?"

Blake's voice cracked out in an oath. "You've gone out of your mind, woman. Do you think I'm going to let a butcher cut up a child of mine? He's no doctor. He's a crook and a skunk."

"You hear that, men?" he called to the posse behind him. "Are you going to stand by and see a little girl murdered?" For a moment there was silence behind him, then a voice spoke up hesitant, dubious. "Well, I dunno, Blake—I've heard tell this Grimson is a pretty good sawbones. Red Murphy was…."

"You've heard tell!" a harsh voice cut him off, menacingly. Alma thought she recognized it as belonging to one of Bogart's hired gunmen. "You've heard a lot, haven't you? If he's a doctor why ain't he practicing at it? That's what I want to know. A sawbones, eh! Sawin' safe doors is about all he's good for!"

Blake said: "Can't you see it's a trick, boys? They pulled in there because one of them is hurt. I shot him when he was getting out of the bank. They thought we'd never think to look for 'em here. And now they're wiling to murder a little child to cover themselves up and get a chance to ride for it. That's all. Well, I'm Julie's legal father and I'm not going to stand for it."

"Sure!" called another voice behind him. "Let 'em give their-selves up or take what's comin' to 'em."

A number of voices yelled agreement. "If it hadn't been for them the little girl wouldn't have been hurt."

"They're killers. What do they care if it's a baby they kill!"

"Let's get 'em!"

Blake said sharply: "Come out of there, Alma, and bring Julie with you. If those yellow skunks have got a scrap of decency left, they won't hide behind a woman's skirts."

"No, listen, *please*—" Alma began.

Blake cut her off. "We've listened enough. If you won't come out, then get out of the way—because we're coming in!"

"I don't think you'll find it right convenient, Blake." It was Lance who drawled that from the window.

Blake's answer was to fling a snap-shot in the direction of the voice.

As though the report of his Colt was a signal, fire began from the sides and back of the house where men had not heard what was going on or had not seen Alma in the doorway.

Lance's six-gun laced the night with flame as he fired at the flash of Blake's gun. Then the guns behind Blake began to speak, slinging lead, not at the doorway but at the shuttered windows of the living room.

FOR A second Alma stood stunned, unbelieving. She had not thought for a moment that this could happen. She knew the men of Tarpaulin, knew them for decent generous men who would as soon think of subjecting a woman to fire as they would of stealing a blind man's horse. What she had not counted on was the influence of the hired gunmen who would back Blake's hand in everything, and the fear which kept the others from wanting to oppose Bogart or any of Bogart's henchmen. No doubt that if those men were confronted with a clear-cut decision of their consciences, they would find the courage to buck the established order, but Blake's cleverness, she realized, had kept this from being a clear-cut case. As long as there was a possibility of persuading themselves that they were fighting to keep a child from being harmed they would do so—they preferred that to setting themselves against Blake and the power he represented.

While the beginning of this realization was racing through her mind she felt a hard, firm hand on her elbow, and she felt herself drawn aside, while the door closed before her.

"It's no use, ma'am," Flint's gentle voice said in her ear. "A sidewinder like that husband of yours don't care nothin' about little children. He wants us, and he'd would trample down a half-dozen Julies to get us."

"Don't you worry none, ma'am," Charlie Parr told her gently. "We're all set for the operation. You go to help Doc and leave the rest to us."

Alma turned then and saw a sight which was to stay in her mind as long as she lived.

While she had been looking out of the door, the men in the room had been busy. In the most protected corner was a barricade made of a heavy oak-topped table, turned on its side, a chest of drawers, the small case that held her treasured books, and other odds and ends of furniture. Behind the barricade was the low table on which Julie lay. From the floor came the dim light of the lamp, and, hanging from the top of the chest of drawers, was a dark-lantern, its rays trained on the bared abdomen of her little girl. In the air was the light, throat-catching smell of chloroform, and there was Doc Grimson in his shirt sleeves, his arms bared, his face in the dim lantern-glow, intent, as he rubbed something from a whisky bottle on Julie's skin.

She realized with a sense of wonder that he had gone on working steadily all the time; realized that he had already administered the anaesthetic; understood that even with the first, sudden hail of lead crashing through the shuttered windows he must have gone on quietly about his task.

In the brief second during which she stood noticing these

details, he looked up, smiled at her encouragingly and motioned her to come.

"Your materials are down on the floor by the lamp," he said, cheerfully. "Suppose you get down there, too."

"But you? You are not protected!"

"I'm sorry, but that's a risk that we must take."

"But couldn't you put Julie on the floor—then you could be down there too—behind all these things," she protested.

Doc Grimson shook his head. "It's too delicate an operation. I'd be afraid to try it on my knees. A surgeon has got to have freedom of movement—and his muscles must be free from strain. Don't think I haven't thought of it—haven't thought that Julie's life depends on my stayin' safe until the operation is done. It's a risk that we've got to take."

"Then," Alma told him passionately, "I'm not going to stay on the floor, in safety, while you're exposed. I'm—"

A curt gesture silenced her. "You'll have plenty of chances to be brave. Never take a risk you don't have to take," he told her quietly. "What good could you do me or your little girl by exposing yourself? You'll have to stand up part of the time—I'll tell you when. Get down now, please, and listen to what I have to say."

She listened, while he gave her directions, told her the uses of the various instruments, bandage rolls, clamps, etc. which were arranged in neat order on the floor.

The firing, she realized, had practically stopped. She wondered why, and as she wondered, she heard Charlie Parr chuckle: "I bet they can't figure out why we ain't shootin' back. They're askin' themselves right now if we ain't sneakin' out some way. I give 'em about ten more shakes to git restive an' start breakin' out in the open."

"What about that arroyo out back?" Lockjaw asked somewhat belatedly. "Can't they sneak up pretty close back there?"

"I wouldn't advise 'em to," Charlie told him drily. "Flint's back there and he's playing for keeps tonight. He's kind of worked up, Flint is. No, I wouldn't like to be the jaspers that tries to sneak up that arroyo tonight."

Lance came in. "They're collectin' over in the brush in front of the house," he said. "Looks like they was goin' to make a rush for it. I reckon I better be here."

ALMA HEARD them only vaguely. She was watching the first swift, sure stroke of Doc Grimson's scalpel as it cut through Julie's skin and she was fighting with all her strength to master the horror and revolt which sickened her.

From the rear a Colt hammered four times in spaced, equal explosions. A sharp, scattering fire replied to it. The Colt spoke again—once—like the period to a sentence.

Charlie Parr grinned. "I was tellin' you, wasn't I?" he remarked.

Alma fought down a wave of nausea and handed Doc Grimson another roll of bandage; watched his swift, supple fingers insert it into the gaping incision.

Charlie Parr swore. "Well, blast me, if they ain't tryin' to sneak up on us!" he exclaimed in disgusted wonderment. "Wigglin' out on their bellies like a lot of danged rattlers!"

Lance said in a low voice which carried to Alma's ears. "Try to pick out Blake."

Lockjaw said: "Shucks! Let's save him until the last and skin him alive!"

"We got to try and get him tonight," Lance replied. "If we don't, Flint's goin' to hunt him down tomorrow and get himself killed. He isn't fast enough for Blake."

"Oh," said Lockjaw comprehending. He peered out through the crack in his shutters. "Wish there was a moon," he muttered after a moment. "A man can't tell who's out there."

"What do you think, Charlie?" Lance asked. "They're in pretty good range."

"Let 'em git in a little," Charlie said testily. "The sooner we shoot the sooner we'll draw fire. Let 'em git in until we can get a fair chance at 'em before they can git back to cover."

Alma listened to them with only half of her mind but heard them in wonder. It seemed to her that she never would get over the fantastic strangeness of that night. The slow, casual voices of these men, coming out of the darkness which surrounded the barricade, came to her like voices in a dream.

Had they really come out of the night, faithfully, to risk their lives for a strange woman and a baby girl? Was it really true that they were surrounded, trapped by half a town, with no slender chance to save themselves, as they spoke to one another with the easy indifference of men at target practice? And this other man, slender, with the guns strapped low on his thighs, and the supple strength of his swift fingers, and his face in the lamp-glow, remote, absorbed, like the face of a priest at some ritual—could he be real?

Lockjaw's voice came up out of the darkness with a sort of

thoughtfulness. "You know," he said slowly. "I bet it's my fault we're in this jackpot. I bet that there danged angle-worm what was in the restaurant, heard what I said and come an' told Blake about it!"

Charlie Parr's outraged snort was an eloquent mixture of despair, disgust, and incredulity.

Lance's voice in reply was a little choked, like a man fighting laughter or some strong emotion—Alma could not tell which. "Don't worry about that, Lockjaw," he said, "it might have happened to anybody."

But there was a lingering overtone of delight, in the words which convinced Alma that it had been mainly laughter, surely, which he had choked down—affectionate laughter, from the gentleness of his reply.

"You think it was my fault, Charlie?" Lockjaw was evidently impressed by that snort. He sounded worried.

"Well, amigo," Charlie's voice was dry, "It did pop up in my mind a few hours ago that maybe that would have something to do with it. But don't you git feelin' bad about that. There's shore one big compensation for havin' you around to git us into jackpots, and that there's the pleasure of bein' in a jackpot with a fellow like you." Alma suddenly could almost see these extraordinarily young blue eyes twinkling in the wrinkled leather of his face.

"You ain't sore, Charlie?" Lockjaw's voice sounded a little relieved.

"Hell, no! Hey! They've come far enough. Let 'em have it!"

And suddenly the room filled with the shocking blast of

heavy Colts and the acrid fumes of burnt powder. Perhaps nine or ten shots in all—echoing, deafening thunder rolling under the low beams of the ceiling. Then stunned, comparative silence, filled only with the staccato bark of the guns out there in the dark, the thud of bullets against the walls, the splintering rip of lead through thin shutters.

A BULLET whined like an outraged bee past Alma's ears and smacked into the wall behind her head. Instinctively, she ducked for shelter behind the barricade. Immediately, her apprehensive glance sought Doc Grimson. The withdrawn expression of his face had not changed. He appeared wholly unaware of the lead that continued to hum spitefully through the shuttered windows.

He seemed to be working deep inside now. Alma dared not look. She felt weak and spent. Somewhere, somehow, she must find the strength to go through with this ordeal. She mustn't faint—must not let herself go even a little. She rested on her knees, hands pressed against her bosom to still the sick tumult within, her eyes fixed on the face of the man who worked on her child. Afterwards—long afterwards—she realized that it had been a posture of worship, and that seemed to her fitting enough.

"Needle—cat gut," he commanded her absently. It came to her in a flash of comprehension, as she handed them swiftly to him, that this man was no country doctor. This was a surgeon, accustomed to the quick, obedient hands of trained nurses. His words, his tone, created in her mind a picture of the operating room of some big city hospital, as she had sometimes imagined it for herself—the cloistered quiet, the white gowned nurses, swift, efficient, alert; the physician, absorbed, remote—high-priest of life and death. She thought that this was perhaps the greatest miracle of all. This man was no cattle-country sawbones, but a surgeon. And the certainty grew on her as she watched the subtle, sure, infinitely delicate movements of his hands, that he was even a great surgeon. How could this have happened? How could he be there, in her lonely little ranch-house, this man—hunted, trapped, bearing the brand of the habitual criminal—this man whose fine gray eyes seemed to gather up the essential light of intelligence itself and whose hands bore this cruel gift of mercy?

Almost, in the wonder of it, she forgot the lead that sang its song of death in her ears. Life, death itself, seemed scarcely important beside the marvel of a world which could show such miracles.

A bullet, ranging down, struck the top of the book-case, ricocheted, with an hysterical scream, to slap against the wall.

Doc Grimson, one hand deep in the incision, reached back, groping, for the dark lantern, brought its rays close to the wound. "Come and hold this for me," he said absently. Then, as she took the lantern with a hand which trembled a little in spite of herself, he seemed to become aware of her again as an individual. "Not long now," he said with an encouraging smile.

Her hand stopped its trembling, steadied. But he seemed unaware of that; that look of remote, intense concentration had come back on his face, and his hands were busy.

Vaguely, she heard the talk of the men around her. The attackers, it appeared, had lost their taste for trying to sneak up on the house in the darkness. They preferred to sit off at a distance and snipe at the windows. The men at the windows, except for occasional glances out, seemed to be squatting on their haunches against the shelter of the walls. Someone came in and put things up behind her and Doc Grimson; afterwards she discovered they were mattresses from the beds. She heard an ironical voice say: "Them boys are sure suckers for the fellows who sell them ammunition," and someone else chuckled. There was some shooting from one of the bedrooms....

But really, she was oblivious now to everything but Julie's wan, drawn, unconscious face and the hands that worked at her body, stitching, clamping bandaging, and the blur of the endless minutes that dragged at her weakness, plucked at nerves which seemed to have nothing left to give.

She heard another voice say sharply, "Look out! Here they come!" Then the deafening, rocking roar of the Colts, and again the crazy whine of lead, like a frantic swarm of insects above her head—bullets knocking like june-bugs against the over-turned table, the chest of drawers, the walls.

Blood spurted in a long streak from Doc Grimson's jaw. He patted the final bandage into place, put his hand in an automatic gesture to his cheek, looked absently at the blood on his fingers, wiped them on a bandage, took Julie's wrist in his other hand, feeling for her pulse. After a moment he said: "She'll do, I think. Give her half a teaspoon of whisky every half hour as soon as she can keep it down, and feed her liquid and raw eggs as often as she can take food. The main thing now is to replace the blood she's lost. Have your local man out to look at her as soon as he gets back."

He gathered his instruments, rolled down his sleeves, slipped into his coat, and said: "All over, boys. What's the program for gettin' out, Charlie?"

He looked like a different man. The cool, amused look had come back into his eyes and his manner was brisk, buoyant. Alma thought incoherently: "They stopped the rush. I must thank them. What can I *say!*"

Charlie Parr said: "The broncs are in the arroyo, Doc. We'll ride into the creek. It overhangs and will give us cover on that side. The creek's deep though, too. Anybody that wants to crack down on us from the low side will have to come close up to the edge. And either I'm wrong, or that will be a mighty discouraging thing to try to do."

Alma tried desperately to thank them, found herself cut off, overwhelmed by the hard, friendly pressure of hands telling her "good-bye, an' good luck, ma'am."

Lockjaw said: "I got your instruments, Doc. Let's go."

She heard their swift, somehow unhurried footsteps troop across the kitchen floor. She dropped on her knees and began to cry as though she would never stop.

CHAPTER 11
"—TO RIDE THE RIVER WITH!"

THEY SLIPPED out and let themselves down into the arroyo where the horses waited. Lockjaw was the last to

97

go down. As he disappeared over the edge he glimpsed a group of perhaps half a dozen men sneaking up on the bedroom side of the house. Evidently they had crept across the wide open space on that side, under cover of the last rush from the main body of the attackers.

The idea came to Lockjaw that Blake must be in that group. What Lance had said about the necessity for keeping Flint from being killed by the marshal had stuck in Lockjaw's head. He had made up his mind at the time that he himself would kill Blake at the first opportunity, thus relieving Flint of the danger he was insisting on running. The absurdity of such an attempt on Lockjaw's part, given the fact that he was considerably slower with a gun than Flint was, did not occur to the slow-thinking outlaw. That was not the way his mental processes operated.

He thought: "I'll go back just for a minute and kill him—then Flint will be all right."

Immediately, he turned and clambered quietly back up the embankment. As he got to the top he saw that one or two of the men were entering the bedroom window. He crossed softly to the kitchen door, entered and went toward the living room. Blake and another man were already there. Alma Blake stood confronting them, one hand clenched at her side, the other holding a small, pearl-handled revolver.

"Talk," Blake was commanding, "and talk fast—if you know what's good for you."

"Never mind the talk," Lockjaw roared, "Go for your gun, you skunk—I'm killin' you!"

The two men spun, cat-like at his first word. It wasn't necessary for Blake to go for his gun. He already held it in his hand, as did Lockjaw, and then they raised their hands to fire at the same instant. At least they began to raise their hands at the same instant. Blake's movement was so much quicker that Lockjaw's gun was still pointing at the floor when the marshal's Colt roared, and a slug smashed into Lockjaw's chest.

The impact of the lead rocked him, but his gun scarcely wavered in its ascent to the level of Blake's heart. It came up, steadied, rock-like.

The gunman with Blake had been standing at the other side of him. Their turning movement had therefore brought him behind the town marshal and he had had to step to one side before he could fire. But even that instant's delay did not handicap him enough to enable Lockjaw to fire first. As the latter's gun came up, trained inexorably on Blake's heart, the gunman's Colt added its blast to the echoes of the town marshal's shot. Lockjaw's six-gun flipped up, bullet-driven, and came to a crashing rest against his own cheek. The blow sent him staggering backwards just as Blake's second shot rang out.

Lockjaw brought up against the door-jamb, dazed and shaking his head like a wounded bull to clear the red mist from his eyes. The black bag containing Doc Grimson's instruments, which he had been carrying all the while under his left arm, dropped with a thud to the floor. Disarmed, shot through the chest, stunned with the welt made by his own gun, it was plain that he was done—finished.

But that was not enough for Blake. Deliberately he trained

his gun on the sagging figure and, to Alma's unbelieving horror, prepared to drive a final bullet through Lockjaw's heart.

Alma Blake never knew what happened within her at that moment. She had no real memory of what she had done. No doubt the instantaneous conflict within her was so violent as to leave no memory. On the one hand, there was the loyalty she had for these men who had risked themselves to save her daughter, plus her growing hatred for Blake; on the other was her whole training.

All she knew afterwards was that she saw her husband stagger, shot, it appeared, in the head. She watched him fall heavily to the floor. Then she found herself looking in bewilderment at the smoking muzzle of the pearl-handled gun in her hand, vaguely conscious that that must have had something to do with Blake's falling.

THE GUNMAN was staring at her in utter surprise, all movement in him momentarily arrested. Suddenly however his head snapped toward the kitchen door, his eyes narrowing viciously, his thumb raking the hammer of his poised gun. Lance Clayton was in the doorway, a gun in each hand. As the gunman's Colt leveled, Lance's right gun roared once. The gunman clutched his stomach and sagged, dropping his weapon. Lance's left gun exploded almost simultaneously. One of Blake's other followers dodged back into the hallway leading to the bedrooms, as the slug ripped a splinter from the door jamb in front of his face.

Lockjaw still stood, dazed, shaking his head. The whole affair had taken place in a matter of racing seconds.

Lance slipped an arm around Lockjaw and half-supporting

him, backed toward the rear door, his right gun menacing the men in the hallway. Charlie Parr met him there and between them they managed to get the wounded man down the embankment.

"It wasn't my fault, Lance," Lockjaw mumbled, "I was just goin' to kill him when that other snake shot my gun out of my hand."

Somebody yelled: "They're in the arroyo! Get 'em."

They rode then, Lance holding Lockjaw in the saddle, feeling his heart contract as the big man sagged helplessly against him. He had been hard hit. It came to Lance that if Lockjaw died this night, it would be as bitter a blow as he had ever thought of.

An insane rattle of fire burst out on all sides at the sound of their horses' hoofs, but the bullets sung harmlessly over the arroyo edge. The main attacking force began to run toward them, hoping to cut in on them as they reached the junction of the arroyo and the creek, but the movement came too late.

There was danger, though, that the posse would arrive before the longriders could reach the shelter of the first jog in the creek and thus be safe from an enfilading fire which, even in the dark would be deadly.

"Set your pace by Lance," Doc said in a voice just loud enough to be heard, "he's holding Lockjaw and can't hurry."

They were riding in single file, keeping under the shelter of the overhanging bank of the creek, their horses splashing along at a trot. Would they make it to the bend before that hell broke loose behind them? Lance felt his backbone crawl and grow cold.

Figures showed themselves on the low side of the creek. Doc's and Charlie's guns crashed in a staccato inferno of welcome. There was the grunting fall of badly hit men, and then the bank was suddenly clear.

The rattle and bark of Colts and Winchesters behind them advised them that the attackers had reached the junction of the creek and arroyo and were sending searching lead down the narrow defile of the creek. But they were beyond the bend now, shielded from that danger.

Shouting, already faint, followed on this burst of fire and they guessed that the others were running for their horses.

"Hold it a minute, Charlie," Doc said coolly, "and let's have a look at Lockjaw. We're not going to make it anyhow, at this rate."

They pulled up while Doc made a blind examination of Lockjaw's wound. After a moment he swore softly. "In the chest," he muttered, "hard to tell how bad it is. Have any trouble breathing, Lockjaw?"

But Lockjaw did not answer. He had fainted.

"We'll have to go at this now," Doc said curtly. "He's losing too much blood. Keep the horses well under the bank. Where the hell is my instrument case with those bandages?"

"Lockjaw had it," Charlie reminded him. "He must have dropped it somewhere."

FLINT TOOK a clean shirt and undershirt from his saddlebags, and with that Doc bound the wound. A group of horsemen, riding hard, pounded by on the lower bank. They rode wide of the creek and did not see the five under the shadow of the overhang.

"Listen," Lance said excitedly. "They're all going to be riding by here like hell on a holiday, thinking that we're foggin' for the open. Let's ride back a little and when we think the last bunch has gone by, cut for town. That'll be the last thing they'll be looking for."

"I ought to have thought of it!" Doc exclaimed softly. "That doctor's away. I noticed his house this afternoon and it looked closed up. If he's a bachelor, we'll hole up there!"

They turned and rode slowly back. Another pound of hoofs, this time on the high side, brought them up, silent as this new bunch of riders streamed by. Presently the five rode on. They had to stop again, several times, for scattered groups, but nobody rode up the creek and nobody stopped to see if they were still there.

Tarpaulin, except for the section that housed the saloons and dance halls, was dark and deserted. Those citizens who had not joined the posse had gone to bed long ago.

Unerringly Doc led them to the physician's house by a back way. There was a barn behind—a small one, but it would conceal their horses.

"Better be sure there's nobody in the house, Doc," Charlie whispered.

"Wait here," Doc told them. He crossed the back yard like a shadow. They heard the slight creak and snap of a window being forced, and then silence.

A few minutes later Doc Grimson's form materialized out of the dark. "Empty!" he whispered jubilantly. "Bring Lockjaw in and put up the horses."

They were barely inside before a group of riders came plodding down the main street on weary mounts.

"Dangedest thing I ever heard of," they heard one say. "Just disappeared! Which, if they ain't got wings, they shore must be moles!"

MORNING FOUND Tarpaulin buzzing with something more than indignation—it was the deep anger with which men meet an outrage upon a child. The report had spread that Julie was dying. Exaggerated tales of the bank robbery, of the serious wounding of several citizens and the death of one, spread from mouth to mouth as mere indignant preludes to the tale of the operation on the little girl. An outlaw—a quack who was not even a doctor—had cut open Blake's child, against his will, and the child was about to die. It was murder!

As to the possible motive, people did not examine it very closely. A report that the act had been one of vengeance against Blake, who had been hot on the outlaw's trail, satisfied most minds.

Alma, hanging anxiously over Julie's bedside, was too preoccupied to correct these rumors even though she had known of them. Jed Pearson, who had slipped out and joined the posse after the fight at the Blake house, attempted to do so, but succeeded only in drawing mob anger on himself. The fury against the five spread without check.

Beginning with the break of dawn, posses pounded out of

town to comb the countryside for some trace of the escaped robbers. Watching them ride past, grim-faced, heavily armed, Lance Clayton, for the first time in his life, could guess what real fear was—fear that perches like a foul vulture, in the pit of the stomach.

He had, in a sense, been hunted ever since that fatal day when gallantry had dictated his comparatively harmless crime for the sake of a lady. But that was different. He and the rest had played a gay game with the law—a game which had as its stakes life and death, it was true but a game, nonetheless. There was something about the aroused fury of law-abiding men, about the grim determination in their eyes and the set of their jaws, which struck, somehow, at the moral bases of his courage. He had a sudden, instinctive certainty that he, with the others, would be hunted down mercilessly by these decent men, until—they were stamped out like so much vermin and his soul shrank within at the thought of it.

For they were trapped! Lance couldn't figure any way out, unless they left Lockjaw. Even that chance was slim now, but it remained their only one. At any hour, at any moment, the doctor whose house they occupied might return. When he did, discovery was certain.

A man on foot came rapidly down the street. His face looked anxious. He turned in at the doctor's house and walked rapidly up to the porch. Lance shrank back from the window. In the inner room, he could hear Lockjaw breathing. The breath came in rasps, heavy and labored.

The man on the porch hammered on the door. Then he called out "Dr. Ed! Dr. Ed!"

Silence. The man hesitated, knocked again on the door, more heavily this time. After a moment he started away, but at the bottom of the steps he paused and looked back at the house. His expression was curious.

Lance thought: "He feels living beings are in this house. It's instinct. His instinct will bring him back here again and again."

An old man came out on the porch of the next house. "He ain't back yit," he called, in the high, somewhat querulous voice of the very old.

"Hullo, Uncle Ike," the man said. "Are you sure?"

"Shore I'm shore—leastways, I ain't seen him. How come you ain't with the posse?"

"The Missus is bad, I dassen't leave her."

"We-ell, I reckon there'll be enough without you. Did you hear if they've struck sign yet?"

"Feller that come in said there was plenty blood in the arroyo back of the house, so I guess one of 'em was hit pretty bad, but there ain't hardly no other sign. The ground got so trampled around there that its hard tellin'. Bogart's sendin' for that Apache over to Navaja Creek and I hear they're gittin' some hounds from Jackson Corners."

"Blood-hounds! Didn't know they was any around here."

"Mighty scarce, I reckon, but there's a feller over to Jackson Corners with a pair of 'em."

"Well, well, well!" the old man marvelled. He sounded pleased. "Oh, they'll git them fellers, all right," he went on, nodding his head with sudden vigor. "They'll git 'em, and when they do they'll tromp on 'em like snakes."

"Killin's too good for them skunks."

"You're right there! If it was me, I'd do like the Injuns used to do—skin 'em and throw 'em onto ant-hills. Goin' around a-stabbin' and a-killin' little children!"

"I got to be gettin' back to the missus," the first man said. He walked away and disappeared down the street. Before he did so, however, he tossed another questioning look over his shoulder at the house.

BLOOD-HOUNDS! DESPITE himself Lance shivered. But they didn't need blood-hounds. Dr. Ed would be bloodhound enough for them. It would be no use trapping him and tying him up. People would have seen him coming down the street, and this house would soon be besieged.

No, it couldn't last. Common sense whispered to him that it would be better to leave Lockjaw and make a break for it. If they were caught here, Lockjaw would die with them. No use sacrificing four men for one who couldn't be saved anyhow.

He felt guilty thinking that, and tried to put the thought away from him.

Doc Grimson came to the door and beckoned him in Dr. Downer's inner office. "How's Lockjaw?" Lance asked.

"He'll live, if he gets proper care."

"That boy's got the constitution of an ox," Lance commented, forcing a grin.

"And the luck of the devil," Doc added. "If he had to get

himself shot square in the chest, he couldn't have picked a better place for the bullet to go through."

Flint and Charlie Parr were in the room. "Find any proof in those papers of Bogart's?" Lance asked, still addressing Doc.

"Plenty—and nothing," he was told. "There's no proof that would go in a court of law, unless we can add to it, but there's enough to convince any impartial man that Bogart's a crook. Ten thousand dollars, for instance, tied up with a rubber band, that I'll give odds belonged to Friendly Joe. A little red account book which shows that Bogart has paid money to plenty of bad hombres. Half the shady characters in the county are on his payroll. And there's some stuff that lets me guess a lot about the disappearance of certain men and the way certain lands came into Bogart's hands. But there's no sure proof, and if we had it, it wouldn't do us any good now. Nobody's going to give us a chance to talk. If Bogart ever gets his hands on us, he'll see that we're strung up before we have time to say anything—and this whole county will help him and applaud him for it."

Lance suppressed a shudder. He had seen a man lynched once. He remembered the overwhelming force of the mob's anger and how it had broken a strong man's nerve so that he had gone to his death groveling and shameful. Death could be faced, but a mob, somehow, could not. He wiped his forehead remembering again the implacable faces of the men who had ridden out of Tarpaulin that morning—after him, this time.

And again the thought rose up in him, stronger now and a little frantic: *there's no sense in sticking here with Lockjaw.*

Doc Grimson spoke, like an echo to his thought. "Flint and

Charlie and I have been talking, Lance—running over the chances we have of getting out of this tight. It boils down to this—if we stay here, we're going to be caught before nightfall. And I don't have to tell you what that means, if we put Lockjaw on a horse, we not only run a chance of killing him, but we make it certain that we'll be run down. No chance of getting out of town without being seen—no chance of getting through a country swarming with men in every direction—unless we can ride almighty fast. It's a hundred to one that if we stay here with Lockjaw, we'll die with him."

Lance could feel the color go out of his face. He wondered if his features were as strained and his eyes as nervous as Flint's were. He started to speak but Doc swept on without giving him a chance.

"Now, I know every one of us hates the thought of running out on Lockjaw. We five have always stuck together. But this time, I've got to admit that it looks foolish. And that's why I'm talking. You've more or less let me be your leader and I've got the responsibility of looking these facts in the face. What I say is this—we can't break up. All four of us have got to stay, or all four of us have got to make a break for it together. If anyone of us has a chance to break through that gang out there, it'll be because we'll be four guns together."

Lance thought: Four guns together—not five. Not five ever again. And a picture came to him of what was going to happen to Lockjaw, even wounded, when that mob got its hands on him.

"In a case like this," Doc went on, "I think that every man

of us has a right to make his own decision and save his life if he can—without fear of what the others will think of him, without any pressure on him, and so I'm going to put it to a vote, and if there's one man who wants to follow his common sense and get out of here, then the rest of us will go with him. What do you say—is that fair?"

"I—I guess it is, Doc," Lance got out.

He forced himself to look at Charlie and Flint. They looked like men condemned to the gallows.

"HERE'S THE way well do it, then," Doc went on impassively. "Every man will take two matches from the kitchen. One of them, he'll light, so the head of it will be black. The other match will have a red head. I'll hold a hat, with a cover over it and every man will put his hand under and drop one of his two matches in the hat. Then we'll take the cover off and look. If there's *one* black match, we'll all make a run for it. And nobody ever needs to know which one of us it was that put the black match in."

"Look here, Doc," Lance asked, desperately seeking some other solution. "Do you reckon that what they say about Julie is true. If she ain't really dyin'...."

Doc shook his head, and the wry twist of his mouth gave his answer before he spoke. "It's no use, Lance," he said. "She's got a good chance to die. I knew that when I operated. It's a question of how much blood she lost. But anyway, it's going to be touch and go for a while yet. She'll look like she's dying—to them. And they aren't going to wait to find out. If she lives, it'll be too late for us."

"Do you think they'll really string Lockjaw up—him hurt the way he is?" Flint asked.

Lance thought: Oh no. They'll just put him on an ant-hill and let the ants walk around in his wound! But nobody answered Flint's question. They just sat there, in silence, avoiding one another's eyes.

"Better get your matches," Doc said, simply.

It fell on Lance's ears like the order for an execution. And that, he thought, was what it was—a death sentence on somebody, on Lockjaw, or on all five of them together.

In silence they filed into the kitchen. In silence, they came back, each man holding in his possession two matches, one with a black head, the other with a red.

Doc Grimson covered his sombrero with a cloth taken from the table.

"You first, Charlie," he said.

Somebody pounded on the front door. The knocking echoed hollowly through the house, urgent, ominous. The four stood still, scarcely breathing. The knocking stopped, and for a moment there was no sound except from the room where Lockjaw slept under the influence of the narcotic Doc Grimson had administered. His breathing, labored and raucous, sounded so loud that Lance thought the man outside must surely hear it.

The old man's voice came from the porch next door. "Doc Ed ain't back yit. I been a-settin' right here on the porch ever since you left, except for just this minute."

The man outside on the porch cursed, despairingly.

From down the street came faint, excited yells, and a moment after, a buckboard clattered down the street at a good pace.

The old man's voice came from next door, shrill now with excitement. "That's them! That's them! Go git 'em, boy! Sic 'em! Sic 'em!"

A dog's bark answered him as the buckboard rolled past—a bark deep-throated and eager, as though the dog responded to the excitement about him. Another dog added his hoarse response to the old man's yell.

The clatter of the buckboard diminished. The hoof-beats of its fast-trotting ponies grew faint in the distance. The four stared at one another, in the eyes of three of them a question, an unspoken surmise.

"Blood-hounds," Lance said, finally. "I heard that they were sending for them."

"Blood-hounds!" Flint Maddox repeated. His eyes were a little wide and there was a sudden unbelieving anguish in them. Lance realized all at once what Flint was feeling. He had been an honest man—a respected citizen, the son of a sternly honest father. And while he had been essentially no less honest for being outside the law, it had nonetheless hurt him, Lance knew, to be considered an outcast by his own kind. And now Flint Maddox, rancher and son of an honored father, was to be hunted to his death with blood-hounds. The thought must have been nearly intolerable to him.

"Blood-hounds!" The words shaped themselves in the silence and obscurity of the room like a tangible horror. Lance wanted suddenly to get out of this darkened and enclosed place at all costs. It wasn't possible to stay a minute longer. He had to have sunlight and the freedom of wide spaces. Nothing else mattered. Nothing! He wanted to yell it out at them. In a moment, the last remnant of his nerve would be gone and he *would* yell it at them. He bit his lip, cursing himself for a yellow skunk.

Doc Grimson said, implacably: "You first, Charlie."

Charlie Parr stuck out a gnarled hand, fumbled to get under the cloth and then withdrew it. His face, creased, leathery, etched in a thousand fine wrinkles, was wooden, impassive.

"Flint."

Flint Maddox shoved a hard, brusque paw under the cloth, the tragic mask of his features molded in a sudden harsh determination.

"Lance."

Lance set his jaw. At least, let me look like a man! he thought. He put out his hand swiftly, saw it disappear under the cloth, opened it, withdrew it.

Doc Grimson put his own hand under the cloth. He hesitated an almost imperceptible fraction of a second before he lifted the cloth aside, like a man whose nerve wavers at the last moment, fearing what he is about to see. Then suddenly the cloth was free and they found themselves staring into the uncovered sombrero.

The four matches in the bottom were tipped with red.

Five they had always been…. Five they would be to the end!

113

CHAPTER 12
THE TRAP IS BAITED

L ANCE CLAYTON turned away quickly to hide the emotion which tugged at his features.

"By God!" said Flint Maddox, "I couldn't have stood it if anybody...." He broke off because it was unnecessary to finish. It was what Lance felt, too. It was what every one of them had feared more, even, than the dog's death which awaited them.

Doc Grimson said: "It was a nasty thing to have to do, but it's all over now. Let's forget it."

His eyes were lighted up with some deep inner glow. He looked like a man who had been reprieved from death, instead of like one who had condemned himself to it. "By God!" he exclaimed, his whole body taut with new purpose. "We'll get out of it yet!"

Charlie Parr looked at him. "You've got a plan," he said quickly. Then, accusingly, "You've had a plan all along, you wall-eyed horned toad!"

"It's not a plan," Doc told him. "It's only a slim chance—the slimmest chance you ever heard of, old-timer. But I think now it'll work. You've given me confidence in it. A bunch of buzzards like you aren't meant to die this way."

"What's the idea, Doc? Get it off your chest."

Doc Grimson raised his head quickly. His keen ears had caught the sound made by a buggy, drawn by a weary nag, as it pulled up in front of the house.

He stepped quickly into the front room and the others

followed, silent, pulses suddenly jumping. They were in time to see a big man get down stiffly from the buggy. His face was grizzled, strong. Weariness etched it in deep lines. He carried a black bag.

As he started up the walk toward the house, the man who had come to the house twice before, came up to the house at a trot.

"Hey! Dr. Ed!" he called. The big man stopped. "Hello, Jim. What's the trouble?"

"It's Annie, Doc. She's bad. I'm afraid…."

Lance held his breath. If the doctor went to see this man's wife, it would be a reprieve—might give them a chance to put Doc Grimson's idea into operation.

"All right, Jim. I'll come over and have a look at her. I've just got to go in and get some things I need—got to go out and see Mrs. Blake's little girl. They tell me…."

"Sure, Doc, that's right," the man interrupted him eagerly. "But couldn't you just come down now for a minute. You can come back here. I'm afraid that…."

"Now, Jim," the big man smiled wearily. "This is the fourth youngster you've had. Aren't you ever going to get over being scared out of a year's growth over it?"

Jim grinned sheepishly. "Well, Doctor Ed…."

"You wait here a minute. I'll be right out."

Lance's heart sank. This was the end!

Doc Grimson said quickly: "Back! Into the office. Close that door into Lockjaw's room."

He, himself, walked softly to the front door and stood behind it, so that its opening would shield him from view.

Dr. Ed Downer came up the steps and put his key in the lock. The other man came into the yard, wandered restlessly around on the walk. From next door the old man called out: "Don't give you no peace, do they, Doc?"

"Hullo, Uncle Ike," Ed Downer's voice boomed. "No, no peace. But then peace isn't so much. There's plenty of it the other side of Jordan, but I don't notice any of us looking for it very hard."

The old man cackled. Dr. Downer opened the door and stepped in. He left it open behind and had taken a pace forward before its closing brought him sharply about. He found himself staring into the muzzle of Doc Grimson's six-gun.

"Don't make any noise," Doc warned him in a low, dangerous voice. "Don't make a sound."

The big man stared at him in astonishment for a second, then comprehension leapt into his eyes. He opened his mouth to speak but closed it again at the warning glint in Doc's eyes. THE MAN outside came up on the porch. Doc Grimson motioned the physician toward his inner office. For a second the big man hesitated. It looked as though he were about to call out, but, whether it was because of the heavy Colt in Doc Grimson's hand or whether it was that he read something in the face of the man who held it, he walked in. His expression did not change on seeing the other men in the room. It was as though he had comprehended and expected them.

Doc Grimson came in and closed the door behind him. "You

can't get away with this," Ed Downer told him, calmly. "You may as well give it up."

"We can get away with it," Doc Grimson told him quietly. "But first, I want you to get rid of that man outside. We intend you no harm, Dr. Downer. And I give you my word that fifteen minutes from now you'll be free to go where you please. But we've got to have those fifteen minutes. Go to the door and tell your friend to go home, that you'll be there in that length of time. I'll be holding a gun on you, and just as surely as you make any break or try to give any information to him, I'll break your spine with a bullet!"

Doc Grimson's eyes were icy cold and his voice carried conviction.

"I'm not sure I believe you, my friend," the other told him indifferently, "but it isn't worth taking a chance on. I'll do as you say."

He walked to the front window and opened it. "I won't be able to get away for a few minutes, Jim," he said. "You go on home and wait for me. I'll be there in fifteen minutes."

"But, Dr. Ed." Jim began to protest, vigorously, but Downer cut him off. "Now, Jim," he said curtly. "Do as I say. I'll be there in fifteen minutes."

He closed the window and walked back into the inner office. As he did so, he took out his watch. "That man lives three minutes from here," he said, looking steadily at Doc Grimson. "In just twelve minutes I'm going to get up and walk out. Make up your mind to that."

Doc Grimson smiled. "We'll make no objection, Doctor," he said pleasantly. "Sit down, won't you?"

Lance looked at him, a dawn of surprised admiration in his eyes. He was beginning to guess what Doc Grimson was getting at.

"Have you heard," Doc asked, when the other physician had seated himself, "what happened here last night?"

"Something of it," Ed Downer replied dryly. "And let me tell you that if you've done anything to harm that little girl of Mrs. Blake's—"

Doc Grimson stopped him with a curt gesture. "We have no time to waste. Listen:" He began then and sketched as briefly as possible the story of their activities in Tarapaulin and the reason for their coming. At the news of Friendly Joe Tarbell's death, the listener swore softly. "You think Bogart had him killed?" he asked.

"I'm morally certain of it."

Dr. Downer looked thoughtful. "Go on," he said.

When Doc Grimson had finished, he looked up. "You say you are a physician," he remarked, his eyes severe. "Are you licensed to practice in this state or any other?"

"No," Doc said, returning his gaze, "I am not. I was licensed to practice, but I no longer am. Why that should be so, doesn't concern us. What I did last night was entirely illegal."

"You have a medical degree, from what school?"

Doc Grimson hesitated. "I prefer not to say," he said slowly. "What difference would it make, if I did? You'd have only my word for it. There's better proof than that what I say is true. Go to Mrs. Blake and ask her the details of the story. Let her tell you the child's symptoms. Then look at the work I did. If you agree that the operation was necessary and that it was competently done, then we can talk further about the situation. I only ask that you do nothing and tell nothing about our presence here until you get back."

"What guarantee have I that you'll be here when I get back?"

"If we meant to try to get away, we'd have done so earlier. We could do so now, by the simple process of knocking you in the head."

Dr. Downer smiled suddenly. "True," he agreed. After a second's thought he asked, "What do you expect me to do? Keep you concealed here? I can't do that. I can't conspire against the law."

DOC GRIMSON'S face was impassive, but the minutest flicker in the back of his luminous gray eyes told Lance that this last statement had struck heavily at his hopes. That, then, had been the crucial point in the game. And they had lost it.

But Doc Grimson was always and essentially the gambler. Nothing of his disappointment showed in his face as he said, calmly, "We can discuss what's to be done when you've come back from the Blake place."

Dr. Downer got to his feet. "I'm going to trust you until then," he said slowly. "All this may be merely a clever lie, but I have no other way to find out. And if your story is true, you've done a fine thing, Grimson—all of you have done a fine thing! You can count on me to help you, in any way that my conscience permits. We'll see."

At the door he turned and asked curiously: "Why did you come here, to my house, last night."

"We had a wounded partner," Doc told him simply. "I had lost my instruments. We had to get him where he could be helped."

Dr. Ed Downer stared. "You mean that you came back into this hornets' nest rather than abandon a wounded partner," he asked.

"Yes."

"And you've stayed here, rather than abandon him?"

"Yes."

The physician whistled softly. "Let me see him," he said, looking at them queerly. Wordlessly, Doc Grimson led the way into the next room, where Lockjaw lay, a great white bandage across his barrel-like chest, his face half-covered with sticking plaster where the gun had smashed him. As they stood looking at him, he opened his eyes, tried, with a grimace of pain, to sit up and then sank back under Doc's restraining hand. "I'd have killed him sure," he muttered, "only—"

"Take it easy, Lockjaw," Doc said softly. Lockjaw closed his eyes and went back to sleep.

Dr. Downer's face was suddenly flushed and his eyes bright. "By God!" he exclaimed softly. "I don't know what else you are, but you're *men*—I'll say that for you!"

When he left the room, his weary stoop had vanished. The spring of energy and determination was in his step.

"Doc," said Charlie Parr, grinning jubilantly. "That's thinking! What comes next."

Doc shook his head. "I don't know, Charlie," he confessed. "We can't stay here until Lockjaw gets well. Five men and five horses are too much to conceal for long in a place like this. I was hoping that Downer would agree to keep Lockjaw here. He might be able to get away with that. Then, come nightfall, the rest of us could ride."

"Wait a minute," Lance said excitedly. "I've got an idea. You convinced this Downer, Doc—why can't we convince this town? To hell with riding! Let's spread this story right. And then let's get Bogart!"

Doc Grimson's eyes flashed. "You got it, Lance!" he exclaimed. "By the Lord, boy, you've got it. I believe we can get Downer to help us. Once people know what actually happened, we can spread the word that we've got the deadwood on Bogart. Once the town's on our side, we'll at least get an even break with our guns. And do we ask any more than that?"

"Hombre!" Lance shouted, his eyes shining, "we do not!"

"I've been knowing right along that I was going to have the pleasure of killing this Bogart," Doc said, "but I wasn't sure just how."

"And I," said Flint grimly, "am sure goin' to fan some happy lead through that Blake's carcass."

Lance's shout had wakened Lockjaw. "No, you ain't, Flint," his voice came sulkily from the bed. "That there Blake is my meat. You leave him be."

"This all sounds pretty fine," observed Charlie Parr drily. "But how do you aim to convince this town? Me, I ain't honin' to go out and make 'em a speech. When them hombres rode out of here this mornin' they shore looked plumb poison bad to me!"

"You're not a politician, Charlie," Doc Grimson told him gayly. "Come on, boys. Dig up some pens and paper. This medical sanctum sanctorum gets to be a printing office from now on!"

CHAPTER 13
HOLED UP

FOR THE next hour and a half Dr. Downer's office was the scene of feverish activity, but as the minutes wore on and Downer did not reappear the nerves of the four men in the room drew more and more taut. They knew that they were racing against time. At any moment some accident might discover them, and if discovery came before they had a chance to put their program into execution, the slim chance which they now appeared to have would disappear entirely. Moreover, Downer was the pivotal point on which that slim chance hung. If his final friendliness had been assumed, or if, through ignorance he decided that Doc's operation on Julie had been unjustified or unskilful....

"You reckon this Downer is all right, Doc?" asked Charlie Parr finally.

"Why, I think so, Charlie."

"He's had time to get back here—unless he happens to be out rounding up a posse to bring with him."

"Hell, Charlie," Lance interjected, "he looked straight as a wagon-tongue to me. He had that man's wife to attend to first."

"I heard somebody tell the old man next door this mornin' that Bogart had put a thousand apiece on our heads. Five thousand simoleons is a lot of *dinero* to a country sawbones."

For a long moment after that there was silence. Each one of them knew that apparently decent men had done worse things for money. After all, Dr. Ed Downer owed them no loyalty. Then Lance Clayton lifted his head, his features suddenly tense. An instant later the others did likewise, listening with held breath. In the distance, toward the edge of town there had risen the deep, baying call of a hound on the trail....

They stared at one another across the table at which they had been working, seeing the hope die out of each other's eyes and desperation take its place.

"I reckon it's the finish," Charlie Parr said at length.

Doc Grimson rose and walked to the window. The old man was still at his post on the porch next door. Aside from him, the street appeared deserted. He turned and stood staring at a small window which gave on the back of the house. Lance knew he was thinking about the horses, guessed that the same thought was in all their minds. The idea of trouble and the idea of a horse were inseparable. And back there, crowded in that small stable were five of the fastest horses in the country—tough, range-bred horses with heart and wind enough to outlast any pursuit.

Beyond in those four narrow walls waited freedom, a fighting chance, the safety that lay beyond the Rio.

"Lance," Doc said grimly after a second, "If you were seen going out now, it wouldn't make much difference. Why don't you slip out and let the broncs go. Give 'em a slap and send 'em down the alley. It—it might throw the posse off the trail a little."

Instinctively, Lance looked at the others. He knew what Doc Grimson was doing, and he was glad of it. There was no chance now of fooling the crowd on their trail—not for more than a few minutes, anyhow. Doc wanted to put the temptation those horses represented finally out of their way. He was burning their bridges behind them.

Charlie Parr nodded. "Good idea. Gives us more time," he said blandly. Flint said: "I'll go with you, Lance."

"No use," Lance told him. "Two of us will just attract more attention."

He went to the back door and opened it. No one was in sight. He walked out to the stable and led the horses out. They snorted with pleasure at being in the open air. Lance expected the old man to come around the edge of the porch at any moment, but nothing happened. He led the horses into the alley, fanned them with a rope's-end and sent them stampeding down the alley. Then he walked back to the house. So far as he could see, no one was watching from the nearby windows. He could hear the hoof-beats of the posse now and voices. The baying of the hounds sounded loud and close. He walked into the house and over to the table where lay the stacked papers they had been working on. He picked them up and walked back to the door.

"It's not much of a chance now," he said, "but I reckon we might as well take it. I'll try and be back for the main performance—so it's no use sayin' 'so-long.'"

"Good idea, Lance," Doc Grimson said. "Might as well do as much as we can."

The others said nothing. They looked at him as he was looking at them—seeing their features, vivid and new, as though they were strangers, but remembering in that moment all the times he had seen them before. He wanted to go in and look at Lockjaw, but he was ashamed to do that. He went out of the front of the house and turned toward the center of town. The old man on the porch stared at him in astonishment.

The posse came pounding down the alley, following the tracks the five had made the night before. In the lead were the hound owner, the Apache tracker, and Bogart. At the barn the hounds showed signs of excitement. One leapt forward, baying, as he came to the place where the fresh horse tracks crossed the old. The other halted, circled, and then ran to the door of the stable, where he whimpered eagerly.

In the house, Doc Grimson slipped his two Colts from their holsters and examined them. Mechanically, Charlie Parr and Flint did the same.

THE SECOND hound got his nose on the fresh scent, followed it to the alley and then leapt after his running mate, baying hoarsely. The posse started to sweep forward after them. The Apache tracker held up his hand. He had been leaning over and examining the new tracks.

"I don' think these horse have men on them. Men stay here— horse go on, I think. Better some men go after dog to find ponies—other men stay here. These track very fresh—three-four minute old."

125

Bogart pulled up and gave brief directions. A dozen of the posse galloped off after the hounds, while the sheriff dismounted and went to the stable door. He looked inside.

"They've been here, all right!" he exclaimed sharply. "Left their horses here all night."

"That's what I call gall!" someone else said in an awed voice. In a moment the yard was alive with dismounted men most of whom went to examine the stable.

"Look! The Injun's right," another man exclaimed. "Their saddles are still here."

Dr. Ed Downer drove up before the house, got out of his buggy and strode up the walk. The old man next door had been peering excitedly around the corner of the porch at the scene in the rear. He was fairly jittery with excitement. Now, seeing the doctor draw up, he hobbled hastily down the steps and ran toward him, calling, "Dr. Ed—wait!"

At almost the same moment the man who had called the doctor for his wife hurried up.

The old man hissed in a loud whisper. "Hey! Don't go in there, Dr. Ed—them robbers are there. I seen one of 'em...."

The big physician turned on him with a ferocious frown. "Are you getting blabber-mouthed in your old age, Uncle Ike? What do you want me to do—quit treating you?"

The old man stared at him, slack-jawed with astonishment. "Why, Ed, I—I, them robbers...."

The other man had come up and was watching the scene with bewilderment.

"You know that if I quit giving you that medicine for your

heart, you'd die in twenty-four hours, don't you?" Ed Downer inquired, with portentous menace in his tone. "You go on back to your porch and set there with your mouth closed as tight as you can get it."

Uncle Ike paled visibly.

"What's this, Dr. Ed?" the other man recovered his tongue enough to ask feebly.

Ed Downer put a powerful hand on his arm and swept him toward the front door. "Come with me," he commanded, somewhat unnecessarily.

He unlocked the front door, shoved the man, Jim, in ahead of him and stepped quickly through, closing the door behind him.

Outside, Uncle Ike had stood staring, as though paralyzed. Now he hobbled swiftly back to his porch, casting bewildered and frightened glances over his shoulder as he went. By what appeared a subconscious reflex, he was holding his lips pressed so tightly together that he appeared to have none.

"Jim," Dr. Ed said swiftly, "I've brought four of your kids into the world, without losing one of them. Now, I'm asking you a favor—will you do it for me?"

Doc Grimson appeared in the doorway, gun in hand. Charlie Parr was behind him. Jim jumped at the sight of them, and began to back toward the door. Doc Grimson leveled the gun. "Don't go," he said.

Jim stopped, shooting a horrified and uncomprehending glance at Dr. Downer. "The doctor was just asking you a favor," Doc Grimson said, significantly.

"Jim," directed the big physician hurriedly. "Get your clothes off and get into bed in my room there. If anybody comes in here, toss around on the pillow and mumble, as though you had fever."

He plunged into his office and emerged carrying a yellow sign. Moving like a whirlwind, he got to the front door, disappeared a moment, and then came back.

Doc Grimson looked at him in sudden comprehension. Then he shook his head. "This is going to be bad, Doctor. You'd better keep clear of it."

"Doctor," said Ed Downer quietly. "I expect I deserve that, but this morning, when I talked like a fool, I had no way of knowing who I was talking to. You'll have to excuse me."

Doc Grimson looked faintly startled.

"No, I don't know your name," Downer reassured him. "I could find out easily enough. There aren't five surgeons alive who could have made that incision. But it's your secret and I'm not going to pry. All I ask is the honor of shaking your hand, sir."

FLINT MADDOX was staring at the pair with his eyes wide, but not Charlie Parr. That old timer never allowed anything, no matter how impressive, to distract him from the business on hand. "Quiet!" he said in a low voice. "They're coming up."

Dr. Downer motioned them back and stepped through the kitchen to the back door. Just as he reached it there was a sharp knock, and Bogart's voice commanded: "Open up!"

Downer swung the door wide, as Bogart leapt sideways, gun

leveled. At sight of the doctor he looked at once surprised and crestfallen. The men behind him looked relieved.

For a second the sheriff did not speak, then he eyed Dr. Downer with the dawn of suspicion in his eyes.

"Ed," he said, "did you know that the five robbers had their horses in your stable all night?"

"I haven't been to the stable," Downer told him calmly, "but I'm not much surprised. Somebody was in this house last night."

"You knew that!" Bogart exclaimed, exasperated. "My God, man! Why didn't you tell anybody?"

Dr. Downer fixed him with his calm stare. "Ben," he drawled, "if you were as busy sheriffing as I am doctoring, you'd maybe understand. In the first place, there was nothing to tell me that the people who were here last night were people who needed to be put in jail—they might have been friends of mine. In the second place, I've had to bring a new little girl into the world this morning and go out to be sure that one that was already in the world wasn't going to go out of it. I've been pretty busy."

"When did you get back, Ed?"

"About two hours ago."

"Did you come here, to the house."

"I did."

"It's a kind of a funny thing, Ed, that those horses were out there until just a few minutes ago. Are you sure the men weren't in your house when you got back?"

"It'd be pretty hard, Ben, for five men to hide in a house this size without my seeing them."

"Yeah," Bogart agreed skeptically. "Pretty hard. Just the same, I think we'll come in and look around."

Dr. Downer's face grew stern. "Just what do you mean by that, Sheriff Bogart," he demanded stiffly.

"Why, nothin' much," the other drawled, "You said that there was evidence that they had been here. I like to come in and look at it—that's all.

One of the men behind him spoke up. "Why, sure, Doctor Ed," he said. "Nobody thinks you'd be protectin' a set of child-murderin' rattlers like that."

Ed Downer swung on him quickly. "You're right, Jud," he said, his eyes beginning to flash. "I'm not in the habit of protecting criminals of any kind. But let me give you a piece of advice. You go after those five men, as stage robbers, or as bank robbers, or as both, and good luck to you! But don't go after them as child-murderers. The man who operated on little Julie Blake last night saved her life. He saved it at the risk of his own because he was first and foremost a physician and true to his oath—true to it right to the center of his heart.

"You want to know how I know? I've just come from Julie Blake's bedside. I had her mother tell me her symptoms and I know from that that she had a hemorrhage of the liver, and had had it for twelve hours—ever since that stage ran over her. I've looked at the work that man did on her and I can tell you that he was no bungling amateur, but a trained surgeon—even a great surgeon. He did a better job than I could have done. He did a better job than anybody I know could have done. Some of you know that I can handle a scalpel, but I tell you that I wouldn't have liked the job of going into that little girl last night. She had lost too much blood. She might have died under a clumsy knife. What you needed then was a man sure enough and fast enough to keep her from losing any more than was necessary during the operation. And that's what that man was.

"And not only that! I've seen the table he worked on and the furniture he piled around the poor little girl to keep her from being hit by the bullets of a lot of hot-headed fools. I've heard the child's mother tell how he himself had to stand up, exposed, while he operated, and I've seen the holes in the wall made by the bullets that whistled around him while he worked. Bank robber? Stage robber? He may be both, for all I know. That's for Ben Bogart and the law to decide. But I can tell you this much, whatever he may be—he's got the hand of a genius and a heart and guts big enough for this whole county! And that last goes for the partners that stood by him while he worked!"

THE EXPRESSIONS of his hearers had passed through astonishment and doubt to wonder, and, as his big voice boomed out the last words, they looked distinctly impressed. For a second, there was silence.

"You—you mean that the Blake kid ain't dyin'?" someone asked at length. The question sounded oddly foolish—inadequate.

"Dyin'!" Dr. Downer snorted. "She's better than anybody has a right to expect she'd be after the accident she had. She'll be on her feet in two weeks."

Ben Bogart's face had lost color and his eyes were burning with fury. "You sound like you felt pretty thick with these hombres, Downer," he sneered. "You're not forgettin', are you, that they robbed the stage and the bank, and killed men doin' it?"

"That's right!" one of the crowd exclaimed. "They killed Fred Jenks and Cherokee Bill and some others are bad hurt." He sounded relieved and reassured.

A rider thundered down the alley and brought up in a cloud of dust. "They've found the horses," he yelled. "They was without saddles or bridles—turned loose— nobody on 'em!"

Bogart swore. "Then they're here!" he exclaimed, grimly. "Downer, I'm searchin' your house."

Ed Downer shook his head. "I'm afraid not, Bogart," he said with equal firmness.

"You think you're going to resist the law, do you?" the sheriff flared, his hand tightening on his gun. "Downer, I'm orderin' you to stand aside and let us in."

Ed Downer shrugged his big shoulders. "You can come in if you want to bad enough," he said. "But I think you better go around by the front way."

"What's this, a trick?"

"Why, no. Leave some of your men here if you want to."

Bogart glared suspiciously. Then he turned to his posse. "Half of you stay here," he directed brusquely. "If anybody tries to get out, shoot to kill! The rest of you come with me!"

Dr. Downer closed the back door and walked around to the front with the others. He gestured to the yellow sign which hung on the front porch. It contained one word only: "Small-pox."

The posse stared and instinctively backed away a little. Bogart's face paled again, but it was obvious that this time anger was not the cause. "What's this?" he asked, still angrily, but in a voice from which the conviction had disappeared. "Another trick?"

"No," Downer said dryly. "It's the same trick. Come in, if you like. The house is free to you."

The sheriff took a step forward, then hesitated. "I haven't heard of any small-pox in town," he said, still staring suspiciously.

"What you've heard, Ben, and what happens to be the fact in the case are two different things," he observed wearily. He straightened and addressed the crowd. "Jim Weston's wife has just had a baby this morning. I've taken Jim in here—because I thought it was best. Anybody that wants to go in and see him is welcome to."

Nobody moved. It was obvious that the sheriff was thinking hard, and also obvious that he had as little stomach as anybody to expose himself to the disease.

"You're tellin' us that Jim Weston's in there—down with small-pox?" he asked finally. "You're givin' your word to that?"

Downer looked at him. "I'm not giving my word to anything," he said contemptuously. "I'm inviting you to look."

BOGART STARED about him uneasily. Then his eye fell on one of the men in the crowd. "You've had small-pox, Lou," he said. "What about you going in and having a look around?"

The man called Lou looked as though the idea did not appeal

to him much. "And git myself shot if them fellers are in there?" he asked.

Ed Downer laughed. "If that's all you're afraid of, Lou—come ahead," he said. "I'll guarantee that you won't get shot."

The man hesitated but finally went reluctantly up the steps.

"How long since you had small-pox. Lou?" Dr. Downer asked. "You know, immunity to it doesn't last forever."

"It's been about seven years," Lou told him uneasily.

Downer pursed his lips. "Oh, well," he said cheerfully, after a moment's thought. "I reckon you'll be all right." There was just the faintest shade of doubt in his voice. "Anyway, we'll have to chance it. Come ahead." He took the man's arm in a friendly way and led him through the door. Lou had begun to sweat a little.

They went down the hallway to Downer's room and the doctor opened the door. Lou moved gingerly over the threshold and cast a glance at the bed. Jim Weston lay there, tossing and moaning. He looked like a man with a high fever.

"Uh—uh—I see," Lou said hastily. He began to back out.

"Satisfied?" Dr. Downer asked him, "or would you like to look under the bed for the bank robbers?"

"N-no," Lou said hurriedly. "Hell, I knew there wasn't nobody here!"

He was sweating more profusely than ever when they got to the porch, but his breathing was visibly easier. "It's all right, boys," he said. "Jim's got it, all right. You can see that!"

Alma Blake's buckboard drew up before the house.

Dr. Downer called out. "You'd better not come in, Alma. I'll bring the medicine out to you." He disappeared into the house and came out in a moment with an envelope which he took out to the waiting woman. She took it, her eyes looking momentarily a little puzzled, and opened it. Inside was a slip of paper which read:

> Go tell your story to as many women as possible. Try to get their husbands to quit the posse.

She said: "Thanks, Dr. Ed," and rode off.

Bogart had been staring, still suspicious. Now, however, he appeared to recall that they were wasting valuable time and erupted into activity.

"I want a dozen men to come with me," he snapped. "We're going to search every house in this town. The rest of you, circle the town and see that nobody goes out of it without my say-so. Half a dozen men will stay here, and keep guard on this house. We'll leave it until last, but if we don't find 'em anywhere else, I'm going to look here—personally!"

He shot a vindictive glance at Ed Downer as he said that.

Downer laughed shortly. "You're always welcome, Ben," he said and went into the house.

Doc Grimson looked up and shook his head. "If I was the poker player you are, Doctor," he grinned, "I'd be a rich man today."

Dr. Downer returned his grin appreciatively. "In my practice, Doctor—" he began, but broke off suddenly. A shot had sounded in the distance, somewhere near the center of town. It was followed by another and another, a sharp fusillade.

CHAPTER 14
MAVERICK SHOWDOWN

L ANCE CLAYTON had strolled down the main street like a man with no purpose and no worries, knowing that if there was a way to escape recognition that was it. No doubt there were half a hundred people in town who had either gotten a good look at him or had glimpsed him, with the other four, as they rode through the streets. But a big percentage of those people—and more especially the crowd in the saloon who had seen him plainly—were out with the posses. Nobody would expect him to be strolling casually about. Even those who would recognize him under other circumstances might not do so now. People, he had learned, usually see only what they were looking for.

He walked first to the post-office. Several older men were grouped on the porch. Lance said, "Mo'nin'." Then with two sharp strokes of his hammer he tacked up two of the slips of paper he had brought with him. The men stared at him curiously as he walked briskly now, over to the front of the general store. When he turned away from there, he could see the men at the post-office grouped in front of the notices he had tacked up. He went on without pause to the sheriff's office, selected three of the slips and put them up there.

Attracted by the noise, one of Bogart's deputies came to the door. He gave Lance one amazed look and started for his gun. But his hand had hardly clasped the butt when he found himself looking into the muzzle of Lance's Colt. He froze.

"Take your gun with your thumb and forefinger and hand it to me," Lance told him quietly.

The deputy, looking a little pale, complied. Lance holstered his Colt, and handed the man his notices, the hammer and tacks. "Walk ahead of me," he said, "and tack these up where I tell you to."

The deputy took them, automatically, but then he pulled himself together. "Damned if I do!" he said angrily.

"Listen," Lance told him, his blue eyes frozen. "I think I'm about to die. I don't like you or any part of you. You do as I say, or I'll drop you in your tracks. It doesn't make any difference to me—except it would be a pleasure."

The man drew a sharp breath and his eyes wavered. He said: "Sure, sure! I'll do what you say," in the soothing tone one would use toward a madman.

Lance put the man's gun in his shirt-front and the two moved off together, the deputy in front. They tacked up notices on lamp posts, on building-fronts, in half a dozen places. Then they came to the Nugget saloon. Lance could see that a crowd had gathered around the group at the post-office and the general store, and groups were forming everywhere the notices had been posted. Men were gesticulating, pointing down the street to where he and the deputy stood.

The deputy tacked up some sheets on the front door of the Nugget. The bartender came to the door. A look flashed between him and the deputy; then the bartender's eyes fell on Lance. He blinked, then tried to look unconcerned and started to turn back into the bar.

"Come back," Lance said. His tone was low but it sounded like steel grinding on steel. The bartender stopped, stared with a sort of terrified fascination at the gaping muzzle of Lance's six-gun.

"Walk with us," Lance said, "or I'll blow a couple of inches off your backbone!"

A grotesque, bandaged figure loomed in the doorway, a heavy .45 in his hand....

The bartender coughed once, hoarsely, and slumped forward onto the bar.

The bartender walked with them. They turned a corner into a side street. As they did so, Lance saw that the crowd was coming down the main street toward them. Not far from the corner, on the side street, was a long, low shed, built off the ground. "Crawl under there," Lance directed the pair in front of him. "Go in as far as you can and don't turn around until I tell you to."

139

They crawled under. The space was low so they crawled with difficulty. Lance watched them until they had gotten well under, then he turned and walked away.

The crowd from the main street reached the corner just then. One of the leaders saw Lance and raised the gun he was carrying in his hand. Lance leapt for the corner of the building, flashing for his Colt as he did so. The other man fired and missed. Lance's gun roared and rocked at almost the same instant. The man dropped, clutching at his thigh.

Lance ducked out of sight as other shots ripped out from the crowd. Then he slipped his gun around the corner and fanned several shots past the ears of the men who had fired. Some of the crowd gave back, but others dropped to the ground to return his shots. He slid back out of sight and turned and ran, just in time to escape a party who had rushed around to take him in the rear. He ran dodging between houses and over fences, with the crowd at his heels. He ran like a startled jack-rabbit, twisting and turning. And he'd have gotten away easily, except for the fact that people, attracted by the firing and the shouts, came to windows, saw him race past, and directed the pursuit.

HE HAD gained a good deal, nonetheless, when he saw a lone man running down a side street which ran at an angle to his course. There was a vacant lot with a fence around it and Lance saw that this man would intercept him at the corner of the fence. He thumbed back the hammer of his gun. Then he recognized Jud Pearson. He remembered that the last time he had seen Jud it was to crack him in the jaw.

They met at the corner. "Hullo, Jud," Lance panted. "Sorry—in a hurry."

"In there—quick!" Jud flung at him. He pointed to the open doorway of a shed which was used as a storage shed but which was now empty. It was a deserted neighborhood. Lance flung a glance around him, saw nobody, and dived into the doorway.

Jud waited until the first of the crowd came plunging into sight, then he yelled, "There he goes!" and ran up the side street, firing his gun. The crowd raced by the shed, turning the corner and following Jud's course.

Lance waited until the stragglers had panted by, then stepped out. Jud Pearson was coming back down the street. "Made out like I fell and hurt my ankle," he explained briefly. "Let's go this way."

"I'm right obliged to you, Jud," Lance told him.

"Want to get you safe so I can smack you down," Jud returned, with an expressionless face, but there was a faint flutter of his left eye-lid as he spoke.

"Thought that might be it."

"Where are the others?"

"Up in Dr. Downer's house. I got to get back there."

"No can do. The posse's there and the house is guarded."

"I got to get back," Lance insisted stubbornly.

When they got to the house, the posse was gone but there were guards in front and back.

"Start limpin'," Jud directed, briefly.

"Jud, you get out of this. You've done plenty."

"Start limpin', jughead, before I tromp you down."

141

Lance said, after a moment's thought, "Gimme me your gun and I will."

Jud looked at him suspiciously. "What for?"

"You're under compulsion," Lance explained. "I've taken your hawgleg and told you to do what I say or I'll draw and kill you before anybody can get to me." He grinned. "That there deputy and the bartender will understand what that means," he added.

Jud handed him his Colt, and they went on to the doctor's house.

"Doctor Ed must have lied his head off for 'em," Jud said reassuringly as they walked. "Anyway, they haven't been taken."

"You don't have to tell me that," Lance grinned. "I haven't heard any sounds of war goin' on."

As they turned in to the doctor's walk a guard stopped them. "Sorry, Jud," he said, "but you can't go in."

"Hullo, Ben," Jud greeted him. "This here's my new rider, Sam Oakley. He's got himself an infected leg, account of him an that outlaw cayuse of mine, Buckbrush, havin' an argument. Sam meet Eb—readin' from left to right, Eben Carter."

Lance shook hands with the guard.

"Dr. Ed in?" Jud asked.

"He went down the street to see what the shootin' was about. You better wait for him here. Jim Weston's in there, down with small-pox." He pointed to the yellow sign.

"Small-pox!" exclaimed Jud. "Say, that's bad. I wouldn't like to have that."

"Man, I mean you wouldn't!" Lance agreed vigorously. "I had it a couple of years ago down in Sonora, and I know."

Carter looked at him in surprise. "You don't look like you'd had it," he remarked. "You ain't got the marks of it on you."

"No," agreed Lance proudly, "not one. I run into a Mex doctor that had some new kind of grease he put on it. Keeps you from havin' scars. Tied my hands down, too. Scratchin' helps to make the scars more than anything."

The guard looked impressed. "That's a new one," he said.

"Yeah," Lance agreed, "but it ain't no joke, all the same. I come so close to dyin' that you couldn't have got a frawg's hair betwixt me and the Other Side."

"As long as you've had it, Sam," suggested Jud, "why don't you go on in and sit down? You ought to get off that leg of yours. I'll wait up town for you."

"Reckon I will," Lance said. "This here prop is sure givin' me hell." And the guard made no objection.

From then on, events in Tarpaulin moved swiftly toward a climax which shook the town to its foundations.

DR. DOWNER'S and Alma Blake's story of what had happened the night before raced from mouth to mouth and in itself produced a sensation. But that sensation was over-shadowed by the excitement which Lance's notices created.

When the crowd which had chased him had a chance to think it over they began to be a little glad that they had missed him. Meanwhile, the main street was thronged with more and more citizens who were eager to get a look at the amazing hints and threats which the tacked-up sheets conveyed. The first one read:

143

The five so-called robbers are in town—well-hidden. They will be in the Nugget saloon at sunset.

Another declared:

Ben Bogart and his gang of crooks have ruled this county long enough. His time is up.

From then on the accusations grew more specific:

What happened to Bill Simpson and his so-called loyal foreman? Ben Bogart got Simpson's ranch on a mortgage when Simpson mysteriously disappeared. Bogart's secret account book shows that the foreman was on his pay-roll and got a thousand dollars in a lump sum the day *after* they both disappeared!

Friendly Joe Tarbell wrote us that Bogart had robbed him of $10,000. He said he had just gotten the deadwood on Bogart, but feared death if Bogart found out he knew. When we got here, Friendly Joe was dead from a knife wound in the throat. Who murdered Friendly Joe Tarbell? Was it Bogart's hired Mexican knife-thrower?

We robbed the bank to get the evidence against Bogart. Nothing else was touched, although the big vault was easier to open than Bogart's private vault. We got the evidence. Tonight, at sundown, this town can see and examine it.

If Bogart and his pet gun-slingers will be in the Nugget at sundown, they'll have a chance to arrest us. This goes for Marshal Blake, who is just as crooked as Bogart, but has fewer brains.

There were others, but these samples give the general tenor

of the campaign. Tarpaulin read them and gasped. The town hummed and buzzed with gossip and speculation as it never had before.

Ben Bogart raged. He stormed up and down town, tearing up the notices whenever he could get his hands on them, denying the charges as the fabricated lies of murderers, fighting to save their unworthy skins. He doubled the reward he had offered for their capture and attempted to press the search for them even more vigorously than before. But mysteriously the searchers drifted away.

Tarpaulin, though it feared him, had secretly chafed under Bogart's rule for a long time. A surprising number of people discovered that these charges confirmed their own private suspicions. They preferred to do nothing to prevent the showdown which was promised for sunset.

Everything Bogart did, moreover, made a bad impression. His snarling rages, his ruthless entry of houses where he suspected the outlaws might be hiding, his attempts to tear up and suppress the charges against him. No one dared to brave him openly, but the sympathy of the town shifted rapidly away from him. Then the housewives who had listened to Alma Blake began to get in their work, and before long the small amount of cooperation which the sheriff was able to command, diminished to the vanishing point, transformed itself into a passive but determined resistance.

A hefty, strong-jawed woman marched down the street to where the guards were stationed before Dr. Downer's house, and there singled out one of them, her husband, for a spirited attack.

"Aren't you ashamed of yourself, Eben Carter?" she opened on him with indignation. "Trying to run down those poor men who saved little Julie Blake's life! Just because they broke into that horrid Ben Bogart's vault! A whole mob of you! It's perfectly cowardly, that's what it is! I'm mortified to find my husband in with such a crowd!"

"Now, Evangeline, you said yourself this mornin'—"

"That's right! Try to blame it on me! As though it was my fault if people go around telling awful lies. You just stop talkin' foolishness, Eb Carter, and come home with me!"

Eb resisted for the moment, but it was noticeable that before long he was missing from his post, and one by one the others drifted away also.

As sunset neared, Bogart spread the word that he would be in the Golden Nugget saloon to meet and arrest the outlaws, in the event that they showed up. But he warned all and sundry that they were desperate and dangerous men, capable of any sort of trickery and that they should be shot on sight. The rewards for them still held, he declared, dead or alive.

"Wants to get them dry-gulched before he has to face their guns," Jud Pearson told himself bitterly, and he determined not only to warn them but also to take his place at their sides in the gun-fight which was to come. His discretion, however, in trying to approach the Downer house from the rear cost him his chance to do either. For as he worked his way toward the back door, the four, Lance and Doc, Charlie and Flint, stepped out the front.

IT WAS a sight for which Tarpaulin was on the alert and waiting. The sidewalks were jammed. People crowded the windows of the buildings up and down the main street. The more reckless among the men were packed into the Nugget, manoeuvering for positions of comparative safety. Seated at a table against the wall, so that they could command both doors were Bogart, Blake, and five of their hired gun-fighters—

Blake's head was bandaged where a bullet had creased his scalp, in the fight at his ranch, it was presumed. No one but Lance Clayton knew definitely that that bullet had come from the barrel of Alma Blake's pearl-handled gun.

So it was that Tarpaulin waited when, just as the last level rays of the sun touched the roof-tops, four figures emerged from the Downer house, traversed the walk, and turned toward the center of town. They walked down the middle of the main street, abreast and in silence. They walked with hats pulled low against the setting sun and each of them wore two guns, strapped low on his thighs.

They walked in silence, eyes straight ahead of them, and silence greeted them as they passed. But no hidden rifle spoke, and no man reached for his six-gun. Perhaps those who craved blood-money sensed the temper of the crowd too well to risk murder; maybe there was something in the manner of these men and in the set of those eight, low-hung guns which was enough to discourage bounty-hunting ambitions.

But behind them a murmur rose—a murmur of question, of comment, of surmise that came on the air like a sudden wind:

"That one in black is the doctor who operated on the little Blake girl! You can't tell me those are outlaws."

"Hell, ma'am—they're four of the most famous outlaws between here and Canada."

"There'll be at least seven against 'em."

"Yep. Seven to four—and two of the seven are Bogart and Blake!"

The murmur rose, died down into stunned silence, rose again louder than before. For behind this steadily marching quartette staggered a strange figure, alone. A big barrel-chested man he was who weaved clumsily, like a drunk, and whose dumb, horse-long face held the look of blind, vacant concentration with which a drunk tries to control his erratic movements. He was hatless and shirtless and bare-footed. From a waist on which the muscles stood out like moving steel cables, depended a non-descript pair of pants, somewhat too short for him. His face was half-concealed under sticking plaster and circling his enormous chest was a great, white bandage on which a red stain grew like a blossoming rose. He wore no gunbelt, but the knuckles of his right hand were white around the handle of a forty-five.

In front of the four, as they neared the Golden Nugget, a man detached himself from the crowd which lined the sidewalks and darted toward the saloon door. The out-stretched foot of someone in the crowd sent him sprawling. Before he could recover himself, the man who had tripped him, yanked him to his feet and gave him a shove in the direction from which he had come.

"Git back!" he snapped. "Bogart'll have all the warnin' he needs when they step through the door."

A menacing growl of approval greeted this statement. Hearing it, another man who had started for the saloon door thought better of his idea and remained where he was.

The four came on, turned in toward the wide, swinging doors of the saloon, and stepped through.

Inside the Nugget Bogart leapt to his feet, his henchmen with him. Two of their chairs fell over with a clatter that crashed on nerves in the sudden silence.

The crowd which had packed itself in to see the performance appeared to wish suddenly that it weren't there.

THE FOUR mavericks had come in without any appearance of hurry but swiftly, nonetheless. Now, after one swift glance around the room, they lined up, facing the sheriff and his crowd. The celerity with which the men behind them had moved out of range convinced them that Bogart had not tried to divide his forces and take them from the rear.

"Your time's come, Bogart," Doc Grimson's voice rang out, harsh and vibrant. "I'm killing you for killing Friendly Joe Tarbell. Fill your hand."

Bogart stood motionless. He had not drawn. The four had been in the door before he had gotten out of his chair. Unable to judge whether or not his henchmen could easily get to their guns, he had waited. Perhaps he had expected some talk that would enable him to get the advantage. If so, Doc Grimson's savage and immediate attack had destroyed this hope. Some such thoughts appeared to race through his mind during that second of immobility. Then he said "Now!" to his men, as his hands raced holsterward and the blued barrels came up with a dull, brief flash like driven pistons.

But incredibly fast as that lead-slinging appeared to the onlookers, the guns across the room had been faster. Doc Grimson's hands had flicked like lizard's tongues; had come up with the speed of light. Lance Clayton had paid no attention to Bogart. His eyes were fixed on Blake, for Flint was directly opposite the marshal. Flint had seen to that the moment they came into the room—and had sent his challenging gaze, like a blow in the face, across the room to the thin, blond man with the half-breed holsters.

He had stood with his arms tingling strangely and his eyes fixed on the marshal's hands. Then, before he himself realized that the things had started, Lance's guns were out, and for the first time in his life he had equalled Doc Grimson's magic draw.

Ben Bogart's body twitched, gave backward, just that fatal instant before his guns exploded, and the snarling lead went wide. Blake sagged, gave to his knees, his eyes insane with hatred.

There was not a man in that epic fight who was not an experienced gunman, and not an unhit man, therefore stood still after those first lightning shots. Not a man, either, who was not doing some wild shooting under the savage pressure of that speed and danger.

Bogart and Blake were hit. They looked mortally hit, but

both had the venomous will of the true gun-fighter. Neither would stop shooting until the heart had stopped its beat and the breath in them had taken its final flight. Staggering, but still erect, Bogart thumbed his guns like a cold madman. Blake, on his knees, still shot from his holsters, his colorless eyes glaring their need to take his enemies to hell with him.

The gunman opposite Charlie Parr had fallen forward on his face, shot through the heart in that first terrific volley. The old-timer had leapt aside to the swinging door, and now lay on his belly, using the door jamb as a shield.

Flint crouched against the bar and sent lead tearing fiercely into Blake's body. Incredibly that thin and riddled torso kept erect, and the marshal's eyes, filmed now, but still smoking their venomous hatred, turned, found this new enemy. The guns roared, rocked, exploded again, but this time the lead searched the ceiling. Blake was dead, still erect on his knees.

Lance had jumped backward to a table, hurled it on its side, crouched behind it.

Doc Grimson had gone to his knees in the middle of the floor, shot through the thigh. But his eyes were frozen, deadly pools, and his guns spat ceaseless death for Bogart.

Another gunman was down. Lance's searching lead had ranged upward through his skull. Bogart toppled forward, riddled. Three left—slit-eyed fighters, pouring lead.

And then three things happened at once. A Mexican holding a throwing knife crept along the partition which continued the bend of the bar, crouching. Almost at the same instant, the bartender popped up from behind the bar and trained a double-barrelled shotgun on Doc Grimson's back. Cross-eyed, pasty-faced, the man was hideous with fear and venom. But the hands which held the shot-gun were steady, and the finger was tightening ruthlessly on the trigger.

THEN THE third thing happened—happened in the form of a grotesque and bandaged figure which loomed through the smoke in the doorway, face set in fierce concentration, hand clutching a Colt .45. The heavy six-gun came up, steadied, and added its booming voice to the din.

The bartender coughed once, hoarsely, like a man with croup, and slumped forward onto the bar, the scatter-gun, still unfired, beneath him.

The Mexican had come crouching and he had not seen this new figure in the doorway. Now he raised, knife poised for the throw. Lance was the target this time. Lockjaw's six-gun leveled again, slow, implacable. The Mexican's knife sailed feebly out onto the floor. Its owner went to his knees, slid forward on his face and lay still.

One of the other gunmen was down now, hand clutching a shattered hip. Two left against five. It would have been suicide for those two to keep fighting. They both realized it at the same moment—their guns clattered to the floor, their hands shot above heads.

"Lockjaw, dang your dumb soul, git off of my leg," said Charlie Parr. "What the hell do you mean by gittin' up anyway?"

Lockjaw grinned at him happily and toppled to the floor, unconscious.

Doc Grimson hobbled over to him anxiously, examined him swiftly. "Loss of blood," he pronounced briefly. "Guess he'll do."

He paid no attention to his own wound, but went at once to the others. Charlie Parr's white hair was stained scarlet from a crease in the scalp which had stunned him and put him out of the fight for ten seconds. Flint Maddox had a flesh wound in his arm. Lance Clayton's cheek streamed blood where a bullet had furrowed it. Not even Doc, shot through the thigh, was disabled.

And then the crowd from outside rushed in, to share a little of the glory of those bolder spirits who had been in the saloon and who had seen a gun-fight which they would tell about for the rest of the days of their lives.

THEY CARRIED Lockjaw back to Dr. Downer's house on a stretcher that day, but they swept the other four up on their shoulders and made a triumphal procession of it through the streets. Tarpaulin had found some heroes and had been delivered from tyranny that day, and it meant the world to know about it.

Half the people in town lined the sidewalks and yelled and cheered until they were hoarse, while the other half marched around and around, carrying four struggling, embarrassed men above them.

Lance Clayton, his face a fiery red, grinned at Doc Grimson as an eddy in the crowd brought them together.

"Doc," he said, weakly, "this is the first time I ever saw you look like a danged fool!"